"Maybe we skip the small talk," Drew said, "and you tell me what's on your mind."

Janet decided to take him at his word. "Look, I'm glad the preschool's getting an overhaul. But that doesn't change the fact that Middleburg's problem is about to become prime-time entertainment."

"You don't trust us to get the job done right."

"As a matter of fact, yes."

"Well, Janet Bishop, I'll make you a deal." Drew pulled out a checkbook and wrote out a check. "This here's a blank check made out to your store. After we're gone, if plaster cracks, if the pipes leak, we'll cover the cost for anything the church needs to order. I don't want you all to feel we've taken advantage of Middleburg in any way."

Janet stared at the check.

"I believe in what I do, Janet, and I mean to prove it to you." He extended his hand. "Will you let me?"

Books by Allie Pleiter

Love Inspired

My So-Called Love Life
The Perfect Blend
*Bluegrass Hero
*Bluegrass Courtship

*Kentucky Corners

Steeple Hill Books

Bad Heiress Day
Queen Esther & the
  Second Graders of Doom

Love Inspired Historical

Masked by Moonlight

ALLIE PLEITER

Enthusiastic but slightly untidy mother of two, RITA® Award finalist Allie Pleiter writes both fiction and nonfiction. An avid knitter and non-reformed chocoholic, she spends her days writing books, drinking coffee and finding new ways to avoid housework. Allie grew up in Connecticut, holds a BS in Speech from Northwestern University, and spent fifteen years in the field of professional fund-raising. She lives with her husband, children and a Havanese dog named Bella in the suburbs of Chicago, Illinois.

Bluegrass Courtship
Allie Pleiter

Steeple
Hill®

Published by Steeple Hill Books™

STEEPLE HILL BOOKS

Steeple
Hill®

Recycling programs
for this product may
not exist in your area.

ISBN-13: 978-0-373-81396-4
ISBN-10: 0-373-81396-1

BLUEGRASS COURTSHIP

Copyright © 2009 by Alyse Stanko Pleiter

www.SteepleHill.com

Printed in U.S.A.

Unless the Lord builds the house,
its builders labor in vain.
Unless the Lord watches over the city,
the watchmen stand guard in vain.
—*Psalms* 127:1

To my late father, Joe Stanko, who built things

Acknowledgments

Returning to Middleburg always means a return trip to charming Midway, Kentucky. Everything good about Middleburg comes from Midway. Everything "quirky" is definitely of my *own* invention. My thanks again to the lovely people—readers included—who've helped me fall in love with this part of the country. I'm so happy to be back and eagerly awaiting my subsequent returns.

My thanks, as always, to my family—especially Mandy and CJ who endured another one of those "research vacations." To the inventors of the DVR, who saved my family from sitting through dozens of *Extreme Makeover: Home Edition* episodes. To Jim Griffin and Alana Ruoso in the art department at Steeple Hill for giving me a delightful cover. And to all of you, for your kindness, your letters and prayers. You are all proof that God can bless abundantly across the airwaves and the miles.

Chapter One

Eight seconds.

Sometimes five, but never more than eight.

Drew Downing knew the world divided itself up into people who loved his television show, and people who hated it. After three seasons of *Missionnovation,* Drew could size up which side of that very thin line any one person stood. Always in under eight seconds after his trademark greeting of "God bless 'ya and hello, Middleburg!"

He didn't need the last five seconds this time... not with the pretty face of that woman in overalls standing at the end of the paint aisle. It broadcast pure skepticism. Drew didn't even need three seconds to tell him Bishop Hardware, while it was Middleburg's only hardware store, would be no instant ally to his cause. "Hostiles," his producer, Charlie Buchanan, called them. Sometimes you could win 'em over, most times no matter what you did they were just sure you had an angle. If the hostiles couldn't find an angle, they never believed you just might not have one. It only meant you hid it well.

Middleburg, Kentucky was the perfect project for the season finale of Drew's *Missionnovation* television renovation program. The tiny town's church preschool had been smashed by one hundred-year-old tree during a summer storm. Toddlers had had to learn their primary colors in the YMCA gym because their preschool had been destroyed. The town had been holding bake sales to buy new roofs and spaghetti dinners to fund drywall. And now *Missionnovation* was here to help.

Some folks at least were glad of it. "My stars!" came a woman's awestruck squeal from over by the gardening supplies. "It's those *Missionnovation* folks! From TV! Pam, look! It's *him.*"

"How may I help you?" The woman in overalls asked.

Wow, Drew thought, I didn't know you could make "How may I help you?" sound unfriendly. "Well, that's just it," he said, turning his gaze to the excited crowd that had pooled into the store behind him, "I'm here to ask you the same thing."

Oh, sure, said the woman's dark eyes. Drew could be in a sea of people thrilled to meet him, and the only thing he'd notice was the one person who was convinced he was on the take. The one person sure the "ministry makeover" *Missionnovation* offered was just too good to be true. Charlie was always giving him a hard time about his obsession to "win over the hostiles."

A chubby older man grabbed his hand and shook it vigorously. "Mr. Downing, we sure are glad to see you and your team here. I'm the one who sent in the application."

"Of course you are." Drew recognized him from the application video and clasped one of the man's shoulders. "And I'm glad you did. You must be Mayor Epson."

"I am." He beamed. A few of the locals patted him on the back. Watching the person who'd sent in the application get to be a hero never got old. That application process was long, complicated and demanded a lot of work. Getting to tell that person their persistence paid off, and their dream project would be realized, and on TV to boot, well that was the high-octane fuel that enabled Drew to pull as many all-nighters as he did.

"Howard Epson, life's about to change. Your town's about to get a shot in the arm like only *Missionnovation* can deliver. Are you up for it?"

These folks watched their Thursday night television. They knew what to do when Drew Downing asked "Are you up for it?" The tiny crowd yelled "We're up for it!" so loud it echoed throughout the store. Two teenage girls grabbed a sheet of paint chip samples off the display next to them and held them out to Drew, asking for autographs. Out of the corner of his eye, Drew caught the lady in the overalls rolling her eyes.

"There'll be plenty of time for that kind of stuff later, gals," Drew said to the pair. "Right now we've got work ahead. You girls think you could convince your classmates to come on over? We need all the hands we can get on demolition day."

"I suppose we can find a few friends," they said. If they were in charge of bringing teens onto the set, Drew knew they'd be the most popular girls in school tomorrow.

"Then I'll put you in charge of teen volunteers. You go see Annie in the bus and she'll get you all set up with a box of T-shirts to give out as you sign folks up, okay?"

"Sure!" They bubbled up the aisle toward Annie, who'd be waiting in the bus as always.

"Mayor Epson, lead the way."

"I'd be delighted!"

Drew turned back to the woman, who hadn't moved from her spot at the end of the paint aisle. He noticed, for the first time, that the name on her Bishop Hardware nametag was Janet Bishop.

Owner? Daughter of owner? Wife of owner? It was too soon to say. "We'll be back later with a mighty long list," he said, pointing right at her.

She looked unconvinced.

Why do hostiles *always* look unconvinced?

Chapter Two

Vern Murphy shuffled up the aisle to stand beside Janet Bishop as she stared after the crowd now leaving Bishop Hardware.

"Don't that beat all," he said, scraping black grease from under his fingernails with the edge of a screwdriver. "He's that TV guy, ain't he? Should spice things up around here for a bit."

"It'll do something, that's for sure." Janet muttered, even though she could hear her father's gravelly voice in the back of her mind saying "Jannybean, if you can't say something nice…"

Vern pointed at the green bus so big it blocked the entire storefront. It had *Missionnovation* across the side in large white letters. "They probably got all kinds of fancy-pants tools in there. You know, like the pneumatic doodads in those catalogues of yours. Might be worth watching.

Sounds like they'll be buying up a storm if nothing else, so business'll be good."

Buses full of tourists were fairly normal in Middleburg, Kentucky. It was a charming, rustic—okay, sometimes a little too rustic—town in the middle of horse country. The kind of town with one main street—Ballad Road—running down the center to comprise its "downtown." A community where everybody knew everyone's name and often everyone's business. Not exactly thriving, but getting by on hard work and watching out for each other. Even so, the storm had hit lots of people hard, and the preschool damage had presented a big challenge. This tourbus, however, was more like a rolling subdivision than your average charter bus. People were already gathered around, talking, pointing, straining to see inside the tinted windows.

"Vern," Janet sighed, "these people have corporate sponsors. Companies who donate everything so they get their stuff on TV. They're not going to need much from us." Janet replaced the can of primer someone had knocked off the shelf in their hurry to follow Downing.

"But he just said he'd be back with a long list," Vern countered.

"A long list of requests, I'd guess. Those people think you'll do anything to get on their show. That you'll fall all over them and give them whatever they want. And we can't afford to be a 'corporate sponsor' right now." She headed back to her office, where she had three orders yet to fill. Actual business, resulting in actual income. She'd have to give Howard a piece of her mind the next time she saw him. He was always pulling stunts like this.

"Sounds like I'd better head on over to that bus and tell them all just what they're dealing with in here," Vern said. "We don't stand for no Hollywood shenanigans."

Ten minutes later, Janet looked up from her order forms to see a short, round-faced woman in a green button-down shirt and glasses standing in her doorway. "I'm Annie Michaels," she said, extending a hand, "vice president of Shenanigan Prevention."

"Um," she stuttered, genuinely shocked that Vern had gone through with it, "I'm Janet Bishop."

Annie cocked her head toward the doorway. "They don't make 'em like Mr. Murphy anymore."

"Vern?" Janet put down the calculator she'd been using and held out her hand. "No, he's definitely one of a kind. Been working here since my dad bought the shop, which means he's been at Bishop Hardware longer than I have."

"He thinks pretty highly of you. He just gave

me an earful about not pulling any fast ones on you. Said you're too smart to fall for any of that…oh, how'd he put it? 'Slick-o TV shenanigans y'all may be used to.'"

"Yep," Janet chuckled, "that'd be our Vern."

Annie pushed her glasses up into her wavy black hair. She had a sensible, friendly smile. "You got a minute?"

"I guess." Janet swept the pile of bulb catalogues off the office's other chair and motioned for her to sit down.

"I meant to come on board the bus," Annie said, "I've got a bunch of stuff I'd like to go over with you, and I can bring it all out here, but…"

But we'd rather deal with you on our turf.

"The sponsors give us so much free food, I'm always trying to share it. Honestly, if I eat one more box of chocolate chip cookies…"

Chocolate chip cookies? Was Janet staring at good fortune or a great background check that they knew her weakness for chocolate chip cookies? Her stomach growled, as if to say it wouldn't quibble much either way. "Well, okay." It wasn't as if there'd be many customers. Everyone in town would probably be at the church preschool by now anyway.

The bus doors folded open with a *whoosh,* and Annie motioned for Janet to step inside. As she walked up the steep stairs, Janet noticed a hand-carved sign hung over the entryway. Home Green Home, it read.

"Drew made that one weekend when it was pouring rain and we were all beyond thankful to have a warm, dry place to sleep. He started calling the bus 'Home Green Home' after that, and it stuck. Granted, though, some days this bus feels less homey than others." Annie shot Janet a look as she turned toward the bus's center table. The bus was high-end; sleek and well-appointed with all kinds of comforts like a microwave, several televisions and plush furnishings. It also had a chaotic, slightly messy feel to it, as papers and videotapes and a few boxes of T-shirts were parked on every available surface. The table, however, was clear and neatly arranged. "Some days a corporate cubicle looks like a positive vacation. Drew's nonstop creativity can be…well, nonstop. But most days this is an amazing job and I thank God for the chances I've got."

Well, thought Janet, *you knew they'd get to the God part sometime.*

As Janet sat down, Annie reached up into a cabinet that was top-to-bottom chocolate chip cookie boxes. And not just any chocolate chip cookie, either. Delicious Dave's Chocolate Chip Cookies—pretty much the finest stuff on the planet.

She'd forgotten that *Missionnovation* had Dave's as one of their sponsors. Every show ended with a parting shot of the whole design team sitting down to milk and cookies with whatever congregation they'd just saved. It was the kind of heavily wholesome scene that made Janet dislike the show, even though her mother watched it every Thursday night she happened to be over for dinner.

"I hope you know your hardware as well as you know your cookies," Annie said as she placed an opened Dave's box on the table and flipped open a thick file of lists. "Drew can come up with some pretty unusual requests." She pulled her glasses out of her hair and put them back on. "Do you want us to just purchase whatever stock you've got, or do you want us to place our special orders through you, too?"

Janet froze with the cookie halfway to her mouth. "You're going to buy your supplies through me?"

Annie looked surprised. "You don't want us to?"

"I'm…" Janet hid her astonishment behind a mouthful of cookie. "I just figured you guys got your stuff through HomeBase." The hardware megastore chain was one of *Missionnovation*'s major sponsors.

"Well, we do loads of business with them, that's true, but we also try to do as much local business as we can."

Annie popped up off her chair and filled a mug from the coffeemaker behind her. Janet noticed a bank of electronic equipment—walkie-talkies, headphones, video-cameras and several machines she couldn't recognize—on a shelf over Annie's head. The woman hoisted her cup Janet's way in a "want some?" gesture, but Janet shook her head. She had never really been the coffee-after-break-fast type. "And, in answer to your question, yes," Annie said as she turned back toward the counter to add a big swig of creamer to her cup. "He really is like that."

"Like what?" Janet hadn't asked a question. Out loud, that is.

"Like what you see on TV. The thing nobody seems able to figure out is that *Missionnovation* is exactly what it looks like. There's no hype or gimmick. Drew and Charlie—that'd be Charlie Buchanan, our producer—just hit on one of those great ideas where everybody wins." Annie sat back down, and Janet wanted to gulp. Had her suspicions been that apparent? "This is a first-class, faith-filled, high-integrity operation, Janet. If you have any problems, even the tiniest one, you come straight to Drew or me, okay?"

I don't know the first thing about you except what I see on TV—that hardly seems enough to go on. Janet stared at the long lists in Annie's hands.

The first page alone had more orders on it than Janet had seen all month. The first file—and there were six—probably doubled all the sales ledgers sitting in her office. If what this Annie said was true, then Bishop Hardware might not have a "slow season" this fall. And that would make a world of difference. Slowly, Janet nodded. "I'd be a fool not to take you up on it."

"Good. I'm glad we got that out of the way. We're the real deal, Janet." Annie dunked a cookie into her coffee. "And you can take that to the bank. We'll try never to give you a reason to worry."

They were just going over the third file when a noise rose up outside the bus and the doors pushed open.

"Annie," came Drew Downing's voice over the crowd, "we got our octopus!"

Chapter Three

"Octopus?" Janet glanced between them.

"Drew, this is Janet Bishop."

"Hi, there." Downing sounded as if he had run the whole way back from the church. "Howard Epson is going to be a handful. Serious octopus."

"The guy who has to have his hand in everything," explained Annie with a wry grin.

"Oh." Janet couldn't suppress a smile. She had an amusing vision of Mayor Howard Epson's ever-present blue cardigan sweater suddenly sprouting six extra sleeves. "Yeah, that sounds like Howard."

Drew used one foot to tug over a stool while he reached into the bus fridge for a bottle of water. "I know he's probably a good guy, but we've got to find something safe—lots of safe somethings—for Mayor Epson to do. I won't get a thing done if he's all over this the way he wants to be."

Annie sighed. "There's an octopus on every project. And it usually is the one who sent in the application. It's great that they feel such a sense of ownership, but…"

"Howard is a bit of an attention and control freak," Janet offered.

"Being elected for three straight terms as Mayor of Middleburg does *not* qualify you to run a bulldozer." Drew gulped down some water before continuing. "He *can't* be the guy to knock down the gym. You need certification to do that sort of thing. Try and talk to him again, will you, Annie?"

"And that," said Annie, gathering up a clipboard, "is the other part of my job. Shenanigan Prevention and Octopus Wrangler. Put *that* on a business card."

"Shenanigan?" Drew looked at Janet.

"Long story," Janet answered dryly.

"You two finish going over that list. I'll go deal with His Honor." Annie snagged her coffee mug—a green mug with the white *Missionnovation* logo on both sides—and headed out the door.

"I'm Drew," Downing said as he extended a hand. She thought it was funny that he introduced himself—everyone knew who he was. Janet noticed his watch was a combination of a snazzy face and a rugged leather band. "And you've met Annie. You got any trouble—any concerns at all—

you bring 'em to one of us. We aim to do right around here."

"So I keep hearing," Janet replied.

"Well," Drew said, shucking off his coat and tossing it on the couch behind him, "if you don't mind my saying so, you looked a bit skeptical back there in the store." He took another swig of water and pulled Annie's file of lists over in front of him. "So you're the Bishop in Bishop's Hardware?"

"That'd be me."

He cocked his head to one side and eyed her. He had brown hair, shot through with a smattering of very hip-looking blond streaks. He sported an expensive brand of athletic shoes, but they'd definitely seen a lot of wear. His jeans were one of those expensive brands, too, but they had rips in both knees and a streak of paint down one side. Still the kind of man better suited for some slick California café than a Kentucky diner. There was no arguing he had a face worthy of television— tawny complexion, strong jaw, killer dimples. The color of his eyes wasn't that noteworthy—it was mostly the gigawatt intensity that made Janet look twice. "You don't see too many female owners in the hardware business," he offered. "Especially in small towns. How'd you get into it?"

Janet was well aware of her uniqueness. Even though she'd been around the store for years, contractors all over the county gave her a hard time when she first took over, testing to see if she really knew her stuff. And she did. Janet knew the name of every type of screwdriver by the time she was three. She was mixing paint by the time she was ten, and could recommend the proper pipe fitting by the time she could drive. "Genetically," she replied. "My dad owned the store."

"My dad was a plumber," Drew said as he dug his hand into the box of cookies and pulled out two. Janet could see the memory overtake him, diffuse the light in his eyes. "He wouldn't know what to make of what I do now."

"Was?" She just knew by the way he said it.

"He died four years ago, just before we signed the deal for *Missionnovation.* Your dad like how you run the store?"

"He's been gone for a couple of years now. I like to think he'd be fine with how it's going."

Drew raised an eyebrow. "You're old enough to have been running a hardware store for five years? Don't they have child labor laws in Kentucky?"

Janet crossed her arms and tried to look every one of her twenty-eight years. "They teach you that in Hollywood charm school?"

"Okay, so maybe we skip the charming small talk and you tell me what's really on your mind. I like it better that way, anyway."

Janet decided to take him at his word. "Look, I'm glad the preschool's getting an overhaul. We needed it, even before the oak tree went through the roof. And I know the school and church'll get all kinds of bells and whistles that they'd never get any other way. And this," she tapped the files between them on the table, "is a whole lot of business for me, that's true. But all that doesn't change the fact that Middleburg's problem is about to become prime-time entertainment."

"Because you don't trust us to get the job done right. You're afraid we'll manufacture drama. Exploit your hardship." He pushed up the sleeves of his green *Missionnovation* sweatshirt.

"As a matter of fact, yes."

"Well, Janet." He leaned forward in his seat. "I'll make you a deal. You won't *have* to trust me. I'm giving you full access. Inspect any of the construction at any time of the day or night." He stood up and went over to a little office built next to where all the electronics stood. "Here are the direct lines to our production staff and our accountants. Call anyone you like to confirm anything you hear from me." He handed her a paper while he pulled open a cabinet revealing a safe. Opening it, he pulled out a fat checkbook.

"I, however," he sat back down again, "am going to trust you from this very moment." He pointed to the file. "There's a list of what we'll need so far. That's only the beginning, of course, but it should keep you busy while we set about finishing the job that oak tree started." He pulled a check from the checkbook and wrote it out to Bishop Hardware, signed it, but left the amount blank. "And this here's a blank check made out to your store. We want satisfied customers. This check is for you to make any repairs or modifications you find you need after we're gone. If the plaster cracks, fix it. If the pipes leak, call a plumber. We'll cover your costs for anything you need to fix that you think was our doing. I don't want you to feel we've taken advantage of you or Middleburg in any way."

Janet stared at the check, filled—except for the "in the amount of" line—with Downing's large, flamboyant handwriting. He'd signed his name so large it overshot the signature line on either side.

"I was raised to be a man of my word. I believe in what I do. I'm the real deal, Janet Bishop, and I mean to prove it to you." He extended his hand with something near fire in his eyes. "Will you let me?"

Chapter Four

"Can you believe it?"

"Hi, Mom."

Barbara Bishop, "Bebe" to her close friends, rushed into the store. "I saw the bus out front even before Sandy Burnside called me at the library." Janet's mother read books for the pre-school story hour every Wednesday. It didn't take much imagination to picture *Goodnight Moon* coming to a screaming halt once word of *Mission-novation*'s arrival hit the streets. Bebe Bishop was a big fan, and part of the reason Janet ended up watching the spectacle every other Thursday when they had dinner together. Before she heard Howard own up to it, Janet half-suspected her own mother of sending in a tape. "Can you believe it?" Her mother's breathless excitement bounced the words out in short spurts. "I mean, can you really believe it, Jannybean?"

"With that huge bus parked right in front of the store, it's a little hard to ignore."

"I heard he came right in here. Did you meet him? And anyone else? Did you meet Kevin Cooper?" Her small, lean frame was practically vibrating with excitement.

Kevin Cooper was the landscaping expert of the *Missionnovation* team, and a personal favorite of Janet's mother, who was close to her pruning shears and potting soil herself. The trellis of blooming flowers that graced Janet's back deck this summer was copied directly from a *Missionnovation* episode. Janet had the misfortune to mention to her mother during said episode that she had "some spare lumber just like that lying around the shop." Before she knew it, Janet's back deck had its own *Missionnovation*-inspired garden trellis.

"No." Janet hadn't yet seen any of the people she saw on TV except for Downing. Despite her "Shenanigan" title, Annie must be a producer or some such thing because Janet had never seen her on the show. "But Drew Downing was in here."

"I got to meet him," her mother boasted as she unzipped the dark blue canvas Bishop Hardware windbreaker she always wore. It had been Janet's dad's and she had to cuff up the sleeves more than a few times in order to make it fit. "He seems just like he is on the show. A nice fellow. Bit high energy, but of course I knew to expect that. He invited me to the prayer meeting at the bus tonight." She pulled a *Missionnovation Daily Devotional* booklet out of one of the jacket's interior pockets. "They don't ever show those on TV, but I read about them. And now we get to be part of it. It's just amazing. Even you have to think this is amazing. After all we've been through trying to raise enough money to fix that preschool?"

"It's gonna be something, that's for sure."

Her mother shot her one of her looks. That "oh, stop being such a wet blanket" look she always gave Janet when she got all worked up about something church-related. Janet no longer did the bubbly religion thing. She told herself she respected the Almighty enough not to try and fake Him out after all she'd seen.

"No prayer meeting," Janet said before her mom even had a chance to ask. "I'll see enough of those folks during the day."

"They're ordering through the store, aren't they? I hadn't even thought about that. Should be a whole lot of business. God's been kind to you. You think about that." She tapped her green brochure on Janet's arm. "You may want to think about giving Him another chance one of these days." Another look.

It was an exchange they'd had far too often. A few years back, Tony Donalds, the son of Middleburg Community Church's pastor at the time, had pulled Janet into a serious relationship. It had been a whirlwind of newly energized faith with the promise of future adventure. And it had opened up facets of Janet's relationship with God she'd never discovered before.

It just hadn't been real. Because Tony hadn't been real.

Janet didn't blame Pastor Donalds—now the former pastor, of course—for not seeing his son's true nature. Tony'd fooled them all. He'd been traveling to raise funds—and then home to raise Janet's hopes—for a mission project that never existed. To capture it in a tired cliché, Tony took the money and ran.

They'd been ring-shopping, hoping to announce their engagement within the month, when it all unraveled. While her mom thought of it as God saving Janet in the nick of time, Janet saw it differently. She'd seen how false "the God's honest truth" could be, and she had every right to put permanent distance between herself and the church.

"Did you hear?" Dinah Hopkins's voice pulled Janet from her thoughts. Dinah owned the Taste and See Bakery just up the street, and she had become Janet's close friend since moving in just over a year ago. It had started out over Dinah's outstanding chocolate chip cookies and grown into a close friendship between the two businesswomen. And even though Dinah was as "bubbly churchy" as Janet's mother, somehow their differences never came between them. Janet was glad for the diversion—until she saw the green-and-white bandana tied around Dinah's wrist.

"Dinah," Bebe cooed, "you been prayin' for God to send you the man of your dreams? I know you've got a thing for that wild Drew Downing—and now he's right here in Middleburg."

"I took one look at that fine lookin' man and thought 'my stars, but he's a blessin' to the universe.'" Dinah sported the remains of a fierce Jersey accent, so such southernisms sounded ridiculous the way she said them. It always made Janet's mother laugh, which is why Dinah fired up the Southern twang every time she was with Bebe. Dinah and Janet's mom were too much alike. Janet, Dinah and Emily Montague, who owned the bath shop up the street, were Middleburg's three single female shopkeepers. Although with Emily's new engagement to horse farmer Gil Sorrent, it'd be down to two single shopkeepers soon.

While Dinah often scouted potential mates, being single didn't really bother Janet. Lots of women were happily single well into their forties, much less their thirties. Life was much kinder to an independent woman now than it had been in her mother's day.

"You didn't already take Drew Downing a plate of cookies, did you?" Dinah wasn't exactly known for her shy, retiring nature. While she'd never admit it openly, Janet liked the many crazy adventures Dinah made for the shopkeeper trio. Dinah didn't always, however, know where to draw the line. "You're not that shameless." Janet lowered one eyebrow. "Are you?"

Dinah winked. "What do you think—'Drew may dig Dave's, but he'll die for Dinah's.'"

Janet rolled her eyes while her mother erupted in a laugh. "Dinah, you didn't."

"I didn't. But I might."

"Don't. I've been in that bus and it has more chocolate chip cookies in it than you've seen in a week. They're in no need of cookies, even yours."

Dinah's eyes grew wide. "You got in the bus? What's it like?"

Janet leaned forward. Her mother and Dinah drew close. Janet waited for dramatic effect, as if choosing just the words powerful enough to describe the iconic *Missionnovation* bus. "It's a bus. It's big. It's green. It rolls. It blocked my front window all afternoon."

Her mother frowned at her. "It's the most exciting thing to happen to Middleburg since I don't know when, they're buying a truckload of lumber and supplies from you and you still can't let yourself get into the spirit of the thing. Honestly, Janet, I wish you'd find a way to stop being such a cynic."

Dinah deepened her voice and flexed a bicep. "It takes a hard woman to run a hardware store in hard times. Good thing you've got me to put a little buzz in your beehive." Dinah had a habit of seasoning her speech with odd little metaphors.

"Are we done yet?" Janet walked back toward her office. "I suddenly have eight colors of ceramic tile to order."

"That church has needed new bathrooms since the dawn of time," Bebe said to Dinah as they followed Janet down the aisle.

"You know it. Wow. Drew Downing and *Missionnovation,* right here in Middleburg. I may have to start liking Howard Epson now. Didn't see that coming. So, Mrs. B., you going to the prayer meeting tonight?"

Janet turned. "I thought we were going to the movies tonight, Dinah."

"Yeah, well, that was before Drew Downing

rolled into town. I got all the entertainment I need live and in person. Did you know he plays the guitar? Musician, craftsman *and* hunk. Mercy!" She winked at Bebe. "Do you think he leads the singing at these things?"

"We'll find out."

Janet watched her friend gab away about the virtues of *Missionnovation* as Dinah walked out of the store with Bebe. Leaving her alone. And now Janet would be going to the movies alone, too. The day was just getting better by the moment.

Chapter Five

Drew waved to the audience after he closed the final prayer of the worship service. "Good night everybody, and God bless. We'll see you in the morning. It'll take a truckload of hands to pull that building apart, but you'll love it when we put it back together."

Drew, Kevin and the two other on-screen members of the design team—electrics and utilities expert Mike Overmayer and furnishings guru Jeremy Sutter—stood around for a few minutes, shaking hands and signing autographs. Drew introduced everyone he could to Annie and some of the other offscreen staff no one ever saw. Annie ran from the cameras, but Drew knew it was tiring to be the team member without celebrity status. He couldn't do what he did without Annie, and he liked to see her get credit. Even if she did blush mightily as she signed her name to the back of someone's devotional booklet. As opposed to Jeremy, who offered to sign everyone's.

It was almost ten, but it felt like two in the morning. He recognized the usual first-day combination of jazzed up and worn out. So, while he'd encouraged the town to go home and get a good night's rest, Drew doubted he'd do much more than grab sleep in fits and spurts tonight.

Kevin, no stranger to the nocturnal challenges of Night One, as it was known around the bus, walked up to Drew as the crowd thinned and handed him a travel mug of coffee. Caffeine had long since lost any effect on the pair—it had become more sustenance than stimulant. Annie always joked that coffee and chocolate chip cookies were the official dinner of *Missionnovation.* "So, who is it?" Kevin said under his breath as they waved good-night to the last of the fans and turned toward the bus.

"The octopus?" Drew nodded in thanks as he took a long drink of coffee. "Howard Epson. He showed up within the first hour—I'm amazed he hasn't asked you to let him sod the lawn himself yet."

"Howard, I've met. Definitely one of our finer octo…" He searched for the proper plural noun. "What's the plural of octopus?"

"Ask Annie—she'd know. Octopi?" Drew guessed as the bus doors slid open.

"Yeah, but who is it?"

"Who is who?"

"Who is *whom?* And it's octopoda." Annie corrected as they walked past her head poking up from a box of files.

"The hostile. The person you kept looking for in the crowd tonight—" he nodded toward Annie "—*whom* I'm pretty sure you didn't find. When are you going to stop that? Don't you get that by definition, the hostiles aren't going to show up to the Night One prayer meeting?"

Drew winced. "Was I that obvious?"

"Only to me," Kevin replied.

"And me," Annie added, now triumphantly holding the file she'd evidently been seeking in the enormous box. She straightened up and grabbed her coat. "Y'all can stay up all night and plan your brains out, I'm out of here." Annie, while a bedrock of calm during the day, knew her limits and disappeared at night whenever possible, generally to a local hotel or, in this case, the local bed and breakfast. Kevin and Drew always had the bus, while Jeremy, Mike, and the others slept on-site in a collection of rented trailers. Drew gladly approved Annie's off-site lodging budget—if she came unglued, the rest of them would fall to pieces within the hour.

And they were, officially, on-site. The bus had been moved to the block just south of the church, beside the firehouse just off Middleburg's main road. Close enough to Ballad Road for them to run over and get something when needed—which Drew imagined would more often than not be something from Bishop Hardware—but not enough to become a logjam for local businesses. The fire station was more than happy to have a little of the limelight, and *Missionnovation* had long since learned that strong firefighters came in mighty handy on demolition and move-in day.

Kevin collapsed onto the bus couch. He hit a few buttons on the stereo in the wall beside him, and country music began to play over the bus's sound system. "You still haven't answered me."

"The hardware store owner," Drew said, sitting at the table. "Our hostile is the hardware store owner."

A frown creased Kevin's face. "A bit of a challenge, but you ought to be able to bring him around by the end of the week if not sooner."

"No chance. This is one situation where I cannot bring him around."

Kevin propped himself up on one elbow. "Drew Downing, admitting defeat on Day One? Why?"

"Because he is a *she*. Janet Bishop, owner of

Bishop Hardware and not, it seems, a big fan of *Missionnovation.*"

"Oh, well at least we know it's not genetic," Kevin laughed. "Now I know why Barbara Bishop introduced herself as Janet Bishop's mother like it ought to mean something. Janet may be your hostile, but her mom is definitely a big fan." A smug grin played across Kevin's face. "I'm her favorite member of the design team. Plants rule!"

Kevin was a big, burly guy with a head full of dark brown curls, usually escaping from under a baseball cap worn backward. His role was landscaping and comic relief. If something goofy happened on the show, Kevin was usually behind it. Drew lost count of the number of arguments Kevin had diffused with some joke or prank. They'd split the *Missionnovation* viewer demographic right down the middle—girls loved Drew, moms and grandmas loved Kevin. Drew, of course, lost no opportunity to rub in Kevin's "gray hair" appeal. Kevin, in turn, mocked Drew's "hunk" status every chance he got. Mike and Jeremy wisely stayed out of the rivalry. Mostly because Mike didn't care who liked him, and Jeremy was sure everyone secretly loved him best anyway.

"The hardware store owner, hmm?" Kevin hoisted his feet up on the couch. "That should make things interesting. How you gonna make this work without her cooperation?"

"She's cooperating, just with suspicion."

Kevin rolled his eyes. "Oh, you love the suspicious ones. They're your favorite. You sulked for weeks over that last one."

Drew found a *Missionnovation* bandana sitting on the table behind him and tossed it at his friend. "Don't you have some roots to dig up somewhere? Something to weed?"

Kevin stuffed his hand into the open box of Dave's cookies on the counter beside him. "I'll put her on my prayer list," he said. He yawned and pulled out a handful of cookies. "Trouble is, which one do I pray for…her or you?"

Chapter Six

Kevin had been snoring for an hour in the top bunk when Drew read Charlie's e-mail one more time. Charlie had sent notes from the initial meeting with the network, and it seemed big things were in the works. HomeBase was considering kicking their sponsorship up to a whole new level, and Drew was staring at negotiations for a multi-season, major network deal. Just think of the lives they could touch. The witness they could be. It felt like God had told Drew to fasten his seat belt and hold on for the ride of his life. And it had been such a ride already.

Drew scanned all those complex tables, outlines and numbers, and gave a heartfelt prayer of thanksgiving for Charlie. Stuff like market share, ratings, brand exposure—all this was Charlie's native tongue and he excelled at it.

Even though he knew Charlie prayed mightily over every move he made, Drew still felt antsy. As if he were holding a very large power tool he'd never used before with no manual in sight. Thrilling, but dangerous. *Where are You taking me, Lord? Where are You taking* Missionnovation? *Keep me focused on You and Your plan, will You? We could have all the success in the world, and if You're not in it, it won't matter at all.*

Sawdust.

Nothing on earth smelled like it, hung in the air like it, or stuck to things with the same airy weightlessness as sawdust. The scent struck a deep chord in Janet every time she caught a whiff of it. Sawdust meant Dad and things being built and Saturday mornings sitting on his workbench, still in her pajamas, sipping chocolate milk from a cup with a bendy straw. Watching Dad explain why you measured every piece of wood twice so you never cut it wrong. She practiced her alphabet by drawing letters in the sawdust with her fingers. She played with the curled yellow shavings from her father's woodcutter, assembled leftover bits of wood the way other kids assembled blocks.

It was the smell of sawdust that came to Janet first as she approached the church grounds. And the sounds; sawing, hammering, drilling, the particular tone of wood clunking together. Those noises and smells created one of Janet's favorite feelings. All too often these days, she was buried under inventory and back orders and bookkeeping. And yet she still loved construction. The texture of wood beneath her hands, the smell of shavings, the satisfaction when two things fit together the way they ought to—these things were at the very core of her love for Bishop Hardware. They were what drew her to her own little version of construction—building birdhouses. Janet had turned one of her bedrooms into a workshop to spend her free hours building artful birdhouses. Castles, lighthouses, English cottages and all kinds of buildings became birdhouse styles for her to miniaturize. She was always cutting photographs of interesting houses from magazines, storing up ideas for future birdhouses. Her workroom had half a dozen carefully crafted pieces—some of them taking months to get just right—lined up on a shelf. To cut and feel and shape and join—even on a tiny scale—fed something so basic in her she couldn't even begin to describe it. Dinah always said she "baked to live." Janet's nature was too practical for such an esoteric sense of vocation, and besides, you really baked to eat, didn't you? But when she finished a birdhouse, or on a morning like this, when she walked onto a job site and saw the raw materials coming together to make something so much more than themselves, she could catch a glimpse of what Dinah meant.

Middleburg Community Church, or "MCC" to its congregation, was what most people pictured when they thought of a small-town church. White siding, tall columns on either side of a china-blue front door, nestled up against a hillside with a parking lot that needed serious patching. The little fenced-in yard of the preschool was a muddy mess since the storm. The portion of the church that had housed the school had been a patchwork of make-do and as-we-get-the-funds repairs for weeks, leaving the church looking wounded and bandaged in a collection of tarps.

Janet looked up as she crossed the church lawn to see that the preschool wing of the church was now completely gone. Simply cut right off the end, like a corner off a sheet cake. That side of the building stood neatly swathed in blue plastic tarps nailed down to the remaining walls with strips of lumber so that the unpredictable winds of a Kentucky autumn couldn't snatch them away. People clad in white hard hats swarmed over the site and clustered around members of the design team.

"Hey, look out there!" Janet's astonished reverie was broken by a crew member's hand grabbing her elbow just before she would have tripped over a wiggling black cable. It was then that she noticed the cameras. There must have been six of them, shouldered by a camera crew that poked in and out of the clustered workers. Three of them, naturally, were trained on Drew Downing. One cameraman was trying, as gracefully as possible, to get Howard Epson to move so he could shoot the rest of the community's participation.

And participate they had. As she began to recognize face after face out of the green-shirted crowd, nearly everyone Janet knew in Middleburg was either helping on the site or watching from the sidewalks. The girls Downing had commissioned to recruit the high school had evidently been quite successful—Janet guessed she was looking at the entire senior class. High school seniors up at seven in the morning on a Saturday? Maybe Downing did have the power of the Almighty working on his behalf.

Or, more likely, the glare of the television lights.

As if he'd heard her thoughts, Drew Downing began walking in her direction. With two cameras in tow. *I knew it'd get like this.*

"Did you ever think you'd see a hardware spectacle?" Drew asked, pulling a measuring tape off his tool belt and depositing it on a table beside him with an unceremonious *thunk*. "I love demolition day. It's more fun than anyone should be allowed to have on television."

And that, Janet thought, is just the point. Demolition was serious, even dangerous business. She hoped *Missionnovation* took safety as seriously as entertainment.

"You've come just in time—this ought to be fabulous. Ever pull a wall down before?"

"Yes," Janet said without any hint of excitement.

Drew pointed at her. "With *your bare hands?*" He thrust his hands into a large box to his left and pulled out a white hard hat with the green *Missionnovation* logo. He held it out to Janet.

"C'mon, lend a hand," Downing said, offering the hat with a gigawatt smile. "You might have a bit of fun if you're not careful. But don't worry, we're careful, too." He motioned toward the line of people gathering across from a trio of ropes that were tied to the church's remaining West wall.

"We've decided to replace the church's entire roof for you, too," he said as they began walking. "Kevin's got an idea to create a garden outside the school windows. It'll even have a miniature cistern to retain rainwater. You know, teach the kids about ecology and water preservation."

Okay, perhaps it was a little impressive. The church had been in dire need of structural improvements even back when she was involved, and based on her mom's conversation not much had changed in the years she'd stayed away. "Have you looked into a full system that feeds off all the roof gutters? If you're going to replace the whole roof anyway, why not alter it into a rainwater retrieval system for the entire church?"

He stopped for a moment, taken aback by her suggestion. "We might take a serious look at that. How many other ideas do you have lurking in the back of that head of yours?"

Janet decided not to suppress the smile that crept across her face. "Probably more than you want to hear."

He grinned as he settled a hard hat down onto his own head. "Let's test that theory. After we yank this baby down, that is."

Howard was getting in the way of things, determined to be at the head of the line until Drew handed Howard his megaphone and insisted that only the Mayor could give the command to pull. Now, one should always think twice before handing Howard Epson a megaphone, but he kept his speech down to an endurable thirty seconds before yelling, "One, two, three, pull!"

And, just like Jericho, the wall came a-tumblin' down in what, Janet had to admit, was an enthusiastic but highly controlled manner.

A second team immediately slid a temporary

wall into place that would protect the existing rooms while the framework for the new school wing was constructed. Kevin and Mike walked through the cheering crowd with a collection of bright green crowbars, showing volunteers how to dismantle the fallen lumber and remove the nails. Like happy ants in green T-shirts, volunteers began crawling over the wall, breaking it up and carrying it away. Janet permitted herself a smidge of admiration. They were doing it right.

Until someone started singing. The crowd joined in, and when she caught sight of her mother conducting half the women's guild with a crowbar, Janet walked off, depositing her hard hat on a table with an annoyed grumble.

Vern met her at the door of the hardware store. She took the day's mail from him and pointed back in the direction of the church. "They're *singing*. It's like a scene from *The Sound of Music* over there— people in matching outfits chirping away."

"I can hear 'em," Vern said. He scratched his chin and narrowed his eyes. "What you got against happy people all of a sudden? Maybe it ain't *Sound of Music*. Maybe it's *Snow White* and I'm a'starin' right at Grumpy."

"I am not grumpy."

Vern leaned against the door and adjusted his cap. "You've been a whole truckload of grumpy since those television folks came into town. I know I had my doubts when they got here, but they seem like good folk to me. I watched them set up yesterday. Good work. Maybe we should give them a little more credit for what they're tryin' to do. Ain't no harm if they have a little fun in the process."

Janet's jaw dropped. That was the closest thing to a lecture Vern had given her in ages. He'd eyed her, drug his feet at some of the things she'd asked him to do, muttered under his breath now and then, but never out-and-out told her off like he just did. Given his first suspicions, this sudden outburst baffled her, and she stared at him.

The old man walked toward her. "Yeah, I was worried at first, too. And I know they're a bit much to take. You're sure we could be blinded by shiny lights and free T-shirts. That we'll all be so busy looking at the cameras we won't see them pulling a fast one on us. And I love you for caring so much about this town. But it seems to me that we ought to remember that Drew ain't Tony. And Middleburg has good folk watching over her. So don't go putting it on your shoulders." He reached out and touched her cheek, his lined face folding into a lopsided old grin. "You don't have to hold up the world, Janny-bean. Just Bishop Hardware. And even that you could put down for a time or two if you wanted."

Janet swallowed, caught off-guard by Vern's gesture. "I'm not *that* grumpy, am I?"

He winked, crinkling up his face even more. "You ain't a potful of glee."

Potful of glee? Where'd Vern come up with that crazy image? Dinah? "Vern, I have never been a 'potful of glee', and I'm pretty sure I don't want to be. I think Dinah's sort of got that covered, anyway."

Vern chuckled. "That she does."

Janet sighed and rolled her shoulders. She had been a bundle of knots since *Missionnovation* pulled into town, and Vern was right: the team had yet to give her any grounds to be suspicious. "I suppose I could cut them a little slack. They are trying to do good out there, even if it is bright, shiny, good."

Vern tucked his thumbs under his suspenders. "I reckon you can find a middle ground between grumpy and glee."

Janet was just about to plant a kiss on the old man's cheek when the hardware store door flew open.

"Get a load of these," Dinah shouted, holding a tray of small cakes with green and white glaze. "Muffinnovations!"

Janet rolled her eyes while Vern said under his breath, "Well, then again, maybe you better worry just a little."

Chapter Seven

Janet was walking back from Deacon's Grill with a roast beef sandwich to go when she heard someone yell "Janet!" and saw Drew Downing jogging up the street to catch up with her. Remembering Vern's admonition to give *Missionnovation* a chance, Janet sat down on a bench by the park and waited for Drew to join her. "Go ahead, don't let me keep you from your lunch," he said, motioning toward the sandwich she held in her lap. "That from Deacon's? Everyone has been telling me to eat there."

"They make the best pie in the county," Janet offered. "And a pretty mean roast beef sandwich besides."

"Looks like it. Although I have to say, I'm really much more of a cake and cookie man, myself."

No wonder Dinah had a thing for him. "Then

my friend Dinah Hopkins's Taste and See Bakery is the place you want. You saw the…"

"Muffinnovations?" he chuckled. "I gotta admit, that's a first. Hard to make something that green taste that good. I'm thinking we should post her recipe on the show's Web site, if she'll share."

"Dinah's very big on sharing. And she's very big on *Missionnovation*. She'll be thrilled." Janet took a bite of her sandwich.

"But you're not. Thrilled. Yet," Downing added.

"Believe it or not, Vern gave me a talking-to on how I should 'give y'all the benefit of the doubt.'"

"I just left a list of electrical conduit and wiring with him. We'll be done framing tomorrow and ready to start pulling some of the utilities through the walls. He's a hoot, your Vern. Reminds me a whole lot of my dad."

"I used to call him 'Uncle Vern' when I was little. He's like a member of our family, he's been around for so long."

Downing threw one arm over the bench and settled back against it. "Why'd you leave so quickly yesterday?"

Janet bit back the sharp answer she would have given before Vern's lecture. "Let's just say it was a bit too much glee for me."

"Not used to people singing with power tools?"

That question didn't even need an answer. Janet

decided she might find Drew less annoying if she understood him better. It was worth a shot. "Can I ask you something?"

"I told you you could ask me anything."

"Well, no offense, but how do you keep this whole thing up? Doesn't it exhaust you to be pumped up and on camera all the time?"

Downing pulled back. "People ask me that all the time." He shifted his weight on the bench. "It gets to the point where you don't even see the cameras anymore. They just fade into the landscape for me. Which means, by the way, that I don't pander to them, either. I don't do things especially for the cameras. And here's the thing. People see through the hype. When something's been manufactured for the cameras—which I try to never let happen, by the way—folks can usually tell."

"There's a whole lot of reality TV that would prove you wrong. You can't tell me some of that stuff isn't drummed up for drama's sake."

"Well, now I'd have to agree with you there. Some of that stuff is just plain nuts. But you see—" his gestures grew as he continued "—you just proved my point—people can tell. Truth always feels like truth, even if it takes a while to get there. It's kind of like Howard. Sometimes he has good things to say, good intentions, but you can always tell what's the truth and what's Howard's grandstanding, can't you?"

"I suppose you're right."

"I know there's some real awful stuff out there on the airwaves. I can't speak for what happens on other shows. All I can tell you is that as much as I can, it doesn't happen on *Missionnovation.* I try to be the same Drew Downing on camera as off." He picked at the fraying cuff of the flannel shirt he wore. She noticed half the pocket was ripped off. He was such a visual contradiction: expensive watch but ratty shirts, trendy shoes with paint splattered all over them. "You're not the first person to ask me how I stay 'on' all the time. The truth is that there is no 'on' and it's easy to stay this way because this is who I am. Drew is Drew is Drew." He leaned in and one corner of his mouth curved up into an infectious, dimpled grin. "So how's about a deal. I won't make you sing, if you let me prove to you there's nothing to worry about. I want you to feel free to drop by the site as much as you want."

Janet eyed him as she took another bite of her sandwich. "You already said that. On the bus. Then again at church yesterday."

"I can't help it. Annie says I'm relentless."

Janet laughed in spite of herself. "You are."

"We can be friends, you know. I won't bite you. You can call me Drew and everything."

She laughed again. "You're crazy, Drew."

"Occupational hazard, *Janet*."

"Watch yourself," she found herself kidding back. He seemed to bring out a long lost humor in her. She used to kid all the time with Vern. With her parents. Where had that Janet gone in the last few years?

Drew checked his watch. "I came to ask you to come over to the church at four-thirty this afternoon. Kevin and I are going to talk to some government grant people—see if we can round up some extra funding for that roof and rainwater system you mentioned. I'd like you to be there. Will you?"

So he'd taken her idea seriously. Somehow she hadn't expected that. "Sure. I can be there."

Satisfied, Drew leaned back and looked around the park. "This sure is a pretty little town. Don't see too many of these anymore. So many of the ones that are left are hanging on by their fingernails with half the downtowns boarded up."

Janet took in the scenery herself. It was one of those color-soaked fall days—the kind that made Middleburg look like a life-sized postcard for autumn foliage. "We have our struggles. It's hard to keep a small town up and running these days. The mom and pop stores can barely make ends meet anymore. So many people just shop at the big stores and shopping malls."

"That's why we do all the local purchasing we

can. But the reality of it is that *Missionnovation* needs the big stores, too. We're an expensive proposition. I can't do what I do—what I'm doing for Middleburg—without national brands backing me up. Their dollars let us do things we couldn't do otherwise. But I know things are tough on the little guy. Some days I'm living between a rock and a hard place."

Janet understood the sentiment. Running Bishop Hardware was a daily excursion into the space between a rock and a hard place. Things were tougher than someone like him probably knew.

The bus was a haven of quiet after the noise of the construction site and Drew's back and forth conversation with Janet. He wasn't sure he'd get her to attend the meeting, even if it was about installing the full-scale rainwater system that had been her idea. He knew that if he was going to bring her around he'd have to get her on-site as much as possible. And she wasn't coming around easy, either. She was fighting it every step of the way. He wondered what could be behind such powerful resistance.

Drew poured himself a cup of coffee and let his body fall onto the couch. He'd been up since five this morning, and it'd be after ten when things wound down at the church, now that they had a set of floodlights put up. Once the drywall went up later in the week, there'd be people in that preschool around the clock. He took a few sips of coffee and let his head fall back against the cushions. This job had turned him into a master power-napper, and he'd come to recognize when it was time to shut his body down for a stretch of time. Kevin once told a health magazine that Drew Downing got more sleep in a twenty-minute nap than most people got all night. Things had quieted down for the afternoon, and he was feeling good about getting Janet's participation in the meeting, so now seemed the perfect time for the luxury of a snooze.

As he lay there, waiting for sleep to come, his thoughts remained on Janet. She wasn't a great physical beauty, although her face had feminine, delicate lines. Her short hair suited those memorable cheekbones and enormous brown eyes. There was a clean strength to her appearance, a no-nonsense groundedness to the way she carried herself. If she had a lean or curvy figure, it was hard to tell under those overalls she always wore. As he almost fell asleep, he found himself wondering what she'd look like in a yellow sundress.

Which thrust his eyes wide open. Maybe he needed more sleep than he thought. He usually wasn't the kind to let a woman turn his head on the job.

But it wasn't like that. Not that he didn't find her attractive in an innocent, Audrey Hepburn kind of way, but it was more than that. He admired her.

Which was funny, because really, the thing he most admired about her was how unimpressed she was with him. Janet wasn't swayed by the tidal wave of excitement *Missionnovation* brought to a place. She'd been more worried about the safety of her town than the things *Missionnovation* could do for her store. He'd found those types of unswayed people to be solid and grounded; and she seemed to be—under all that defensiveness. Where had that groundedness—almost a hidden nobleness—come from? She had a strong sense of who she was, yet she seemed selfless, too. Janet Bishop, he guessed, would be the kind of person to make a big donation to a charity, but do it anonymously.

When you asked Janet a question, you'd get an honest answer, even if it wasn't the answer you wanted. In the kiss up media world, those kind of people were few and far between.

What have You got going on with her, Lord? he prayed as he slumped down farther into the couch, sleep starting to overtake him. In his experience, that kind of full-out honesty grew out of some experience with deception. He wondered if that were true with her. *Where did all that suspicion*

*come from? Any plans on doing away with some
of it while we're here?*

Why was that his problem? Sure, she was a
"hostile," and that instantly put her on Drew's
radar. But somehow Janet Bishop wasn't the
ordinary "hostile." With most of the reluctant
types, Drew just cared that they liked the show. It
was more personal with Janet. Mostly because
she was somehow making it personal. While she'd
never really voiced it, he got the strong impression that she was not so much suspicious of *Missionnovation* as she was suspicious of *him.*
Unconvinced of his integrity.

That was it, wasn't it? He could handle
anyone's suspicions of the show—he had a thick
skin where *Missionnovation* was concerned—but
it was bugging him that Janet Bishop wasn't
willing to take him at his word.

And that was a sore spot, because he *was*
feeling the squeeze in the integrity department
lately. Success was a funny thing in this business.
Instead of making things easier, it made things
more complicated. Bigger deals had more strings.
Success bred expectations of more success. You
could mess up when you were small potatoes, and
people would just brush themselves off and go on.
Trip up when everyone's watching, and suddenly
the mishaps grew harder to put behind you.

As the projects had met with success and the show had grown over the first three seasons, people began to take notice. Media people had recognized that *Missionnovation* was on to something. So it wasn't new that a network had shown interest. Last season, they'd gotten a solid offer or two, promising visibility, production budgets and backing. But all of them made subtle requests for Drew to "dial down the God." To use the word *faith* instead of *Christianity*—things like that. As far as Drew was concerned, that was non-negotiable. *Missionnovation* was about renovating the places where worship happened. And that meant Jesus would be present and accounted for—every episode.

Drew laid his forearm across his face, shutting out the strong afternoon light that came through the bus window. With Kevin's music not on, he could hear the birds. It felt like months since he'd been able to lie down and listen to birds. His life was so full of noise lately that some days it was hard to think straight. To listen. He shut his eyes. *Keep me on the straight and narrow, Jesus. The view's getting fuzzy from up here, and I don't ever want to stray from Your plan for this. Just make it work.*

Make it work.... He prayed over and over as he drifted off.

Chapter Eight

Some unknown time later, Drew felt an insistent tapping on his boot. He opened his eyes to find Annie standing there, clipboard in hand. He wasn't surprised to find a worried look on her face—Annie didn't wake him up for just anything.

"Annie, I know that look," he sighed, pulling himself upright. "Trouble?"

"Depends on your point of view."

Drew rubbed his eyes at the enigmatic answer. "What's up?"

"When you didn't check your e-mail, Charlie sent a fax. Big network meeting next week."

Drew sat up straight when he read the fax. "Next week? He knows I don't leave the site, ever." He stared at the column of names at the bottom of the fax, listing the people to be at the meeting. Names he didn't recognize, but titles that indicated they were dealing with HomeBase's top brass and network heavyweights.

Drew pulled out his cell phone and hit the speed dial for Charlie's private line at the California production office.

Charlie picked up on the first ring. "I knew I'd get your attention with a fax."

"What gives? You get all those bigwigs in one place and you make it the week I can't show up? You sure you can handle all that influence in one room without my supervision?"

"Bingo, Drew. There's a lot of power on that list. Three seasons of huge exposure, huge resources. They have schedules that would choke mere mortals like us. You need to be here."

Drew didn't reply. He thought his *own* schedule was bad enough, but never did understand the subtleties of the network deal—that was Charlie's territory. It probably took Charlie months to set this thing up.

"I know it's not how you'd like it," Charlie continued. "I know you're going have to give a little on the project to be here, but you know me. I wouldn't ask you if it weren't important. Seriously, Drew, we're looking at a once in a lifetime shot here. You need to be in L.A. when this happens."

Drew began pacing the bus. "There's got to be another way. If you've got them all together, and it's that important, let's just spend the money and fly them out here. Let 'em see *Missionnovation* firsthand. This one's a dream—it's the ideal episode for that kind of thing—they'd eat it up."

Drew heard Charlie sigh. "I thought of that already. I proposed it. I even told them I'd charter their flight directly into Lexington and have them home by dinner—eight hours from top to bottom."

"And…"

"No go. It's L.A. or nothing."

Drew ran his hands through his hair. "I hate this. Don't do this to me. Don't ask me to cut corners."

"No one's asking you to cut corners. I can have you in and out in twenty-four hours, and you know you've got people who can handle the site. Drew, we've talked about this. As *Missionnovation* grows, you're going to have to step back a bit from the day-to-day stuff. That's leadership. You've got to be out in front so your people can follow."

Drew caught sight of his reflection in the bus windows. He couldn't quite picture the scraggly lad in front of him doing deals with all those network and corporate heavyweights. This felt more like being backed into a corner than being out in front, leading. Drew had a long history with Charlie, though; long enough to know Charlie only made demands when he had no other choice. "You're not going to ask me to wear a suit or anything, are you?"

Charlie laughed. "Do you even own one?"

"The last suit I wore was to my father's funeral, Chuck. I don't associate them with happy occasions." Drew only used "Chuck" when he was making him mad or pushing his limits. This definitely qualified. Charlie had probably known this was going to be a "Chuck" call before he sent the fax. And he'd sent it anyway. That was Charlie—ready to be "Chuck" if that's what it took to get the deal done. He had to respect that in his longtime partner. "I don't like this," Drew sighed into the phone.

"Welcome to the big leagues. Everything costs a little more up here."

It felt wrong.

"Can I let you know?" he said wearily into the phone. "I need to think about this."

"Think about it. Pray about it. You're free to do whatever it takes to get your head around this. Just as long as you do it in the next twenty-four hours."

And that was television: ponder all you want, but ponder fast. "I'll call you, Chuck," Drew said, and snapped his phone shut.

"What do you think, Annie?" Drew called as he walked to the back of the bus where she'd gone to give him some privacy. "Should I stick it to The Man or do the deal with him?"

"Charles signs my paychecks, but I work for you. I'll back you whatever you decide."

"So you're not going to tell me what I should do?"

Annie pushed her glasses up on top of her head. "Do I look like the kind of girl to take God's job away from Him?"

Janet stood on the church steps watching the government types get back into their car. "You're very smooth, I'll grant you that."

"You know," said Drew as he put a rubber band from his pocket around the blueprints he'd rolled up, "when you say that kind of stuff, it never sounds like a compliment. Can I pour on the charm to move a project forward? Yes, I can. All I did was sell the project to their needs and sensibilities. There's nothing wrong with that."

Janet planted her hands on her hips. She would have stuffed her hands in her pockets, but she'd taken the care to put on something nicer than overalls for a meeting with state officials. It'd been weeks since she'd worn a skirt anyway, and she was looking for an occasion to wear the new boots her mother had bought her for her birthday last month.

It was a brilliant idea to propose the rainwater collection system for a government grant—she'd wished she thought of it herself. Drew, though, had clearly also pushed the project's new TV visibility. It felt like an unfair edge. What about all the other worthy ecological projects that wouldn't get funded just because there was no celebrity to play the high profile card? "You can't seriously believe your celebrity status and the presence of a television camera didn't affect the outcome of that meeting."

Drew looked at her as she started down the steps. "Well, of course it did. But don't you think I'd be foolish not to use that? I didn't deceive anyone—or knock anyone else out of the running for that grant. Everything I said in there was the absolute truth." He began tapping the tube of blueprints against his open palm. "Did I use every asset at my disposal? Sure. Every gift of gab and insight into human nature God's given me? Absolutely." He stopped at the bottom of the steps and turned to look back up at her. "You know, I never did buy into the concept that deep faith turned you into some kind of doormat. That you had to sit around, contemplating the Biblical truths of the universe, waiting for God to bring life to your doorstep. I count on God as much as I know how for this. But I think that includes working as hard as I can to meet the goals I believe He's set before me. Besides—" he started across the sidewalk "—if you must know, I checked, and there aren't any other viable applicants for that pool of funds right now."

Janet followed after him. "Hey, look, I didn't mean to start a fight."

Drew paused, shut his eyes for a moment, and pushed out a breath. "Sorry—I hadn't even realized you hit a nerve there. I'm overreacting here, aren't I?"

It made Janet laugh. "You're wound a bit tight, yeah."

"I think it's part of the job description. Actually, it might be the majority of the job description. You need to be a little bit wacky to do what I do."

"Well, you got the church a full rainwater retrieval system and a new roof—so maybe wacky's got its uses." She pointed to the blueprints. "But this is a whole church roof now, not just the preschool roof. You'll follow the specs, won't you? Take the time to get all the details done right? Roofs are serious. Roofs are supposed to last decades. I'd hate to see the church dealing with leaks in two years' time because someone cut a few corners to make their television deadline and you're long gone into another blockbuster season."

"You can supervise the installation yourself, if you want to. You seem to know more about the rainwater part than anyone else."

Janet crossed her arms over her chest. "Some of us have to earn our living the *un-televised* way. You know, minding the store, all that day-to-day boring stuff?"

"Hey, that Vern looks like a pretty capable guy. He'd probably jump at the chance to be king of Bishop Hardware for a week."

"King of Bishop Hardware. Very clever. You must play lots of chess in your off hours."

Drew applied a confused face. "Off-hours? What are those? I've heard of them somewhere." He checked his watch. "People can go get a slice of pie in their 'off hours,' can't they? As a matter of fact," he went on, pulling Janet in the direction of Ballad Road until she finally erupted in reluctant laughter, "I'm thinking Deacon's is an excellent use of my off-hours. But I couldn't possibly go alone."

Chapter Nine

It was exactly how Drew imagined it. A homey diner with red-and-white checkered tablecloths and white stoneware mugs that were filled with coffee the minute you walked in the door. Laminated single-page menus with the special of the day written on a chalkboard up by the grill. A linoleum floor, and red vinyl stools lined up along the counter. The classic American diner.

A big, boisterous woman with hair piled high on top of her head called out to Janet as she walked in the door, then made a total fuss over Drew as he came in behind her. "Look here, it's our TV star!" she said, rushing to smooth out the tablecloth at what Drew was sure she considered her best booth. "I was hoping you'd come in here sooner or later."

"Well," said Drew as he extended a hand, "I had

about a dozen people tell me I couldn't leave Middleburg without tasting Deacon's pie. If anything tastes as good as it smells in here, I'm not going to be disappointed."

"This is Gina Deacon," Janet said as she slid in opposite Drew. "All the good pies are her doing."

"I'm tickled to see you in here today, you know," Gina said as she filled Drew's and Janet's cups with great-smelling coffee, "'Cuz I been working on a special project in honor of your visit. I been fiddling around with a local specialty, adding some of those cookies you like so much. I call it Milk and Cookies Pie. Got the first one in back right now. Made with a heaping batch of Delicious Dave's and a whole bunch of other good stuff." She flushed and put her hand to her chest. "I'd be honored if you'd give it a taste."

People often gave Drew things, little trinkets, souvenirs and such, but the gifts that were creations—fruits of thoughtfulness and labor—won his heart most of all. Companies gave him things, he had a box of plaques and awards somewhere in the back of the bus, but it was kids' drawings and a handmade *Missionnovation* knit scarf that decorated his desk. He smiled. "I'd be a fool to turn down an opportunity like that."

Gina strutted off to the kitchen to unveil Milk and Cookies Pie. This kind of stuff just never got old for him. People—all individual, unique people—were still the most amazing things God ever created.

He poured a dollop of creamer into his coffee. Actual cream in a little ceramic pitcher, not that semi-liquid non-dairy stuff that came sealed in little plastic cups. When was the last time he'd not had to take his coffee creamer out of the package before he used it? "I've been thinking about the preschool garden. We're onto something with the rain barrels and the little gardening station. I want to turn it into a mini ecology center. Get kids to realize part of seeing God in the world is seeing God in nature."

Janet took her coffee black. He could have guessed that. "I can't see how anyone would argue with that."

"I noticed this great birdhouse in the church-yard—a little replica of the church. Beautifully handcrafted. Do you know who made it? I want to set up a whole neighborhood of those birdhouses to use in the garden. Can't you just see it? Little birdhouses that look like places in Middleburg? We could even have a Bishop Hardware birdhouse. It would help the kids understand that animals are a part of God's world just as much as they are."

Drew has suspected Janet might find the concept a little too artsy, but since it'd support a local artisan, he thought she'd go for it. Now he wasn't sure—she got the most bizarre look on her face, as if she found the subject of birdhouses embarrassing.

"Don't you have people on your team who could build those kinds of things?" she asked.

"Not like that. I looked at it closely. That thing was really well done."

Gina came back with two slices of the gooiest, creamiest-looking concoction he'd ever seen. She must have caught the tail end of their conversation, because she smiled at him as she set the plates down on the table. "Janet's church birdhouse is adorable, isn't it? I've been thinking about asking her to make up a pair of tiny cottages for my niece's baby shower—she's having twins. You know, one pink and one blue—wouldn't that be sweet?"

Now Drew knew what that funny expression was all about. That odd look was Janet Bishop blushing. Even as she stared down at her pie, he could see her face taking on a decidedly pink glow. She wasn't the kind of woman who wore lots of makeup, so he hadn't noticed until she lowered her eyes like that how incredibly long her lashes were. *Wow,* he thought, if the show's makeup artist got a hold of those eyes, they'd knock a guy clear across the room.

"You made that birdhouse, didn't you? You're talented. You've been holding out on me. There's an artist hiding inside all that practicality." He ducked his head until he caught her gaze. "It's an amazing birdhouse. Even you have to know it's amazing." She looked up at him, and her embarrassment tugged something out of him.

"That one was a special case." Her voice had a completely different tone to it.

"So you do have more? Made?"

It seemed like a simple enough question, but it seemed to unnerve her. "A few. It's a hobby, sort of. I sell them at the shop sometimes."

On second thought, Drew mused, those eyes were pretty amazing all on their own. "Will you let us buy everything you've got? Maybe make a few more?"

"Oh." She rolled her eyes. "I don't know."

"She's a talent, our Janet," Gina affirmed, grinning.

"She's right, Janet. It's a gift, not something you hide behind." Janet blushed more, fiddled with her fork. "We won't even show them on camera, if that's what's bothering you. But can't you see how perfect they'd be?" He caught himself applying the charming pressure he wielded so well, and told himself to back off. Janet Bishop was not a button to be pushed. "Just think it over. I really like the birdhouse I've seen, and I'm sure I'll like your other ones. They'd be great. But it's up to you."

Janet managed a slight nod and Drew felt better. "Gina sure does know how to indulge," Janet changed the subject as she surveyed the chocolate-cookie-creamy-peanuty-caramel pie before them. They took bites at the same time, both falling into moans of satisfaction. It was as if Gina Deacon had taken every great dessert in the world and mixed them all together in gooey perfection.

"Delicious Dave would be proud. Maybe even jealous," Drew replied.

Gina waved him off. "Well, you're sweet to say so. Y'all just enjoy yourself."

Drew dug in for a second heaping forkful. "Nobody needs to ask me twice."

Janet sat at her workbench later that night, trying to glue a tiny shutter onto a colonial-style birdhouse. It was painted to look like a brick house, complete with a tiny chimney and a gray slate roof. Diamond-paned windows and sets of small black shutters peeked out around the oval opening in front. This one had come out especially nice. She imagined it mounted on a pole beside all her other houses in a ring around the preschool garden. It would be like an avian neighborhood, just as Drew described.

She liked the idea. The more she thought about it, the more she liked it. But it bothered her, too.

Like everything Drew Downing did, it felt over-
the-top. All her existing houses? She'd donated
that one birdhouse to the church back when she and
God were still on speaking terms. She'd enjoyed
making and donating that one, mostly, she supposed, because it was her idea on her timetable.
She'd had the time to get it just right and to present
it when she was ready and not a minute before.

She doubted it would go that way with Drew.
Downing was an "everything now" kind of guy.
He'd asked for "all she had and maybe a few
more," and that felt so extreme. Asking too much.
Missionnovation was here for a three-week stint,
and then they'd roll off toward their next spectacular feat. Not only would he take all she had, he'd
probably want a dozen more new houses by
Friday, and she couldn't work that way. Her birdhouses were her own private pleasure, not some
new method for Drew Downing to display his
creativity.

She maneuvered the tiny shutter into place and
clamped it tight. Still, it had been flattering to
know how much he liked them. Drew had com-
plimented the church birdhouse before he even
knew it was hers—and much more so once he
did. Her last two were even better than that church
one—her skills had grown a lot since then. He'd
like these. The soft buzz of satisfaction humming

in her chest when she thought about it wouldn't be ignored.

Janet looked up and ran her eyes along the shelves in her workroom, where the eight birdhouses sat lined up in a neat row. Some of them had been there for a while, keeping her company while she made more. She doubted he would abuse them. He wouldn't do something like ask her to make a mini green-and-white *Missionnovation* bus birdhouse…would he? No, it wouldn't be anything as deliberate as that. It would just feel as if she were contributing to the spectacle of it all—a spectacle that rubbed her the wrong way.

Then again, wasn't she contributing to it already? Bishop Hardware was supplying lumber and pipe, nails and screws—why not birdhouses? If he'd asked her to order a dozen birdhouses from one of her supply catalogues, she wouldn't have thought twice about placing the order.

But these birdhouses were personal.

And it bugged her because it was all getting personal. Drew Downing was turning into one of those aggravating people you want to hate but just can't. Was she ready to accept the fact that the nice guy on TV—okay, the God-fearing, high-voltage nice guy—really was just that?

What seems too good to be true usually is. Wasn't that the old saying? Did she know enough about Drew Downing—about who he was and what he believed—to trust him?

The shutter slipped out of its fastening and slid down the side of the birdhouse, leaving a trail of glue in its wake. Janet sighed and wiped off the glue. She was too distracted for this kind of detailed work this evening.

The troublesome thought was, she couldn't ever remember the last time she was too distracted to work.

Chapter Ten

"How are Gil and the guys liking their brush with fame?" Janet said as she folded town council agendas with her friend, Emily, a few days later. Emily's fiancé, Gil, ran Homestretch Farm about ten miles out of town. Paroled offenders lived at the horse farm as part of a unique reform program Gil ran. A big, surly group of young men managed by a big, surly man, "the guys and Gil" had been obvious choices for some of the heavy lifting tasks during the renovation.

"The guys are starstruck," Emily replied, leafing through a stack of bridal magazines as she and Janet babysat the town hall's jam-prone automatic folding machine. "But I think Gil doesn't know what to do with a guy like Drew Downing."

"Don't we all wonder what to do with him?" Janet said, banging the machine with her hand when it stalled. The contraption sputtered, then settled into the task of spitting out the folded papers with a consistent thumping rhythm.

Emily caught the edge in Janet's voice, and raised an eyebrow. "Not a fan of the big green bus? I've heard you talk about that show as if you watched it a lot."

"*Mom* watches that show a lot. I'm a captive audience when I'm over for dinner. Or when Mom tries some new project out on me that she saw on the show."

Emily shot Janet a glance as she took a stack of folded agendas out of the machine's bin and placed them in a box on the counter. "Your back deck trellis is lovely. I want one."

Which was an amusing comment, because it'd be hard to find any more places to put decorations or flowers on the gingerbread cottage where Emily lived. Janet had wondered—more than once—how she was going to add her brand of charm to the huge work-a-day house she'd live in on Homestretch Farm once she and Gil were married. Gil wasn't exactly the flowerbox and cottage garden type. Perhaps it was living proof that opposites really do attract.

"I'll send Mom over as soon as you're married. And it's not the work I object to. From what I can see *Missionnovation* does good work despite how fast they move. It's the hype. You can't go near that site without somebody pointing a camera at your face."

"Oh, I can imagine. Gil told me they were half an hour late for dinner because he couldn't get the guys to step away from the cameras."

Janet let loose a laugh. "The Homestretch guys? Hamming it up for cameras? Now that's entertainment. That show is turning everyone in this town upside down." Her laugh died down. "I wonder if we'll all still be as thrilled when the circus leaves town."

"Don't you think *Missionnovation* is on the up-and-up? They're going to use your rainwater collection idea. And you said yourself, the team's been doing solid work. Even the hardware store is better off with all those orders. I don't see the downside in this." She paused and pointed at Janet. "Except that we may never hear the end of it from Howard."

Janet let the machine finish its batch and then gave it time to cool off before reloading it. She didn't want to have this conversation with Emily over the noise of that thing, anyway. "I know there're dozens of logical reasons why this could be a good thing. But I don't seem to be able to shake my gut feeling on this. If anyone else had asked to buy all my birdhouses and put them up in the church preschool, I might even be fine with it. So why is it bothering me that Drew asked?"

Emily raised an eyebrow. "You didn't tell me he asked for all of them."

"He asked for as many as I can give him. And you know his rush-rush timetable."

"You could do it. If you wanted to."

Janet looked at her. "But do I want to? Pipes and drywall and stuff are one thing. My birdhouses are another. Those are personal, you know? I take a lot of time and care with those."

"Janet, no one's ever pressured you about church before, they're not going to start pressuring you now about your birdhouses. They already have the one you made."

Emily was another of those church people like her mother and Dinah. Janet appreciated Emily's soft touch when it came to church matters—and was one of the few people other than Dinah who knew the full story of Tony's fraud. Emily seemed to understand the scars Janet carried. She still invited Janet to church things, but was fine when Janet declined.

Bebe never gave in so easily. She'd asked Janet again to come to the prayer meeting at the bus—resulting in another near argument when she declined. Did her mother somehow think the famous green bus would suddenly dissolve years of well-grounded resistance? As if those kinds of wounds could be erased by the right cute guy?

When had she come to think of Drew Downing as cute?

The thought must have shown on her face, for Emily responded with the worst possible question. "Janet," she asked, "is this not about church or birdhouses? Is this about Drew Downing?"

This was why she found it hard to be around newly engaged people. They were forever pairing her up. "No."

"You're sure?"

Janet rolled her eyes and flipped the switch to turn the machine on again. It made a whining sound she'd never heard before, but eventually wheezed into action. "The guy is a walking amusement ride—more ups and downs than a roller coaster. I'm having trouble enough just working with him."

"Maybe there's another reason why. A more personal reason?"

"Please. Leave the hero worship to Dinah." Janet fiddled with a knob or two until the whining stopped. "I'm sure the way to that man's heart is through Muffinnovations. Even Gina baked him a pie the other night and made us try it."

Emily put a hand on one hip. "You took Drew Downing to Deacon's for pie?"

Janet lowered her voice to an aggravated growl. "I was *dragged* to Deacon's for pie by Drew Downing. The man's an unstoppable force."

Emily waved a pile of papers like a fan. "So it seems."

Emily got the chance to learn that for herself the next day. Janet was just finishing boxing up some hinges to take over to the site when Emily practically ran into the shop. "I'm asking you," she said as she caught her breath, "as a friend, Janet, don't sell it to them. Don't let Downing do it."

"Do what?"

"Don't you sell him that paint."

"What paint, Emily?"

At which point Drew burst through the door, running as well. Janet decided Emily must be a pretty good runner to have beaten him, for it looked as if they'd raced here. "You're kidding, right?" Drew said as he stalked up the aisle toward Janet. "The church isn't *allowed* to have a green door?"

Emily squared off at Drew right in front of Janet. "No, it isn't. The church door must be blue."

Drew scowled. "Does Howard know that? He's up there making all kinds of suggestions to my team."

"The door's always been blue. The church is

white with a blue door." Emily said it as if it were a law of nature.

"And green is…" Drew said, looking at Janet for an explanation.

"Not blue," Emily said before Janet could even open her mouth.

"Did I mention Emily is chairman of the Preservation Task Force?" Janet offered, trying to put a friendly tone back into this near-argument.

"Oh," said Drew slowly, "so you're *that* Emily. Gil told me I might have a run-in with you before this was over."

Way to put your foot in your mouth, Drew Downing, Janet thought. You've done it now, mister. You're officially beyond my help.

"He said *what?*" Emily shot back. "Just what did Gil say about a 'run-in' with me?" She shifted her weight, and Janet thought both Gil and Drew were about to regret any further comment. Whatsoever.

"Howard was, you know, strongly suggesting some color scheme change for the church exterior. I was asking him who else might need to be in on a decision and…I met Emily here. Who evidently also has…some very strong opinions on the subject…which Howard had not mentioned." Drew was talking in the short, carefully crafted phrases of someone who knows they are in a heap of trouble.

"And Howard, I suppose, was telling you he was the only person who needed to be consulted?" Janet offered. It was possible. Howard was the chair of the Buildings and Grounds committee, and even back when Janet sat on their committee, Howard would often make decisions without committee input.

"Well, you know Howard," Drew explained, running his fingers through his hair. "I didn't really *think* he had the only say, but I didn't think I'd stepped on an exterior semigloss landmine, either."

"Welcome to Middleburg," Janet said to Drew, "where we take our status quo…"

"Our *preservation*," Emily corrected.

"…pretty seriously," Janet finished.

"I can see that," Drew said. "Blue door. Very important. Duly noted. But…um…do you mind if I ask why blue?"

Janet didn't have an answer. Neither, evidently, did Emily, because the only answer she could supply was, "Because the church door has always been blue."

"And in Middleburg," Janet explained as congenially as possible, "that's reason enough. Drew, how about we don't take Howard's word on matters of artistic license here? If it's okay with Emily, I'll be glad to run interference on this, looking over the plans and letting you know

anything I think ought to go before any commit-
tees. I'm sure that's what Gil *meant* to say to
Drew." Janet directed that last comment at Emily,
who was still fuming a bit.

After a moment, and a nudge from Janet,
Emily's stance softened.

"Oh, I'm sure of it." Drew caught on. "Must've
totally misunderstood Gil. There was lots of
banging around us. He did mention he was
excited to be getting married and all. Congratulations, by the way."

"Thank you." Emily softened further. "We're
very happy."

"Actually, Emily, I think Gil was just looking
for you when I left," Drew said. "Something about
taking you to lunch, maybe? Try that Milk and
Cookies Pie Gina dreamed up over at Deacon's.
It's out of this world."

"Well, I'll just head back to the site, then, and
see what Gil's up to with the guys." Emily headed
back up the aisle toward the shop door. "You look
over those plans, Janet, and we'll talk later."

Drew and Janet watched her walk through the
door and up the street. At which point they both
exhaled loudly.

"I actually thought Howard had a good idea.
Green, ecosystems, nature, you know?"

Janet shifted her weight. "Green, which also

just happens to be *Missionnovation's* signature color, *you know?"*

Drew balked. "I wasn't thinking of that. Really. Oh boy, I wasn't thinking at all, was I?" He shook his head. "How'd I miss that? No wonder she looked at me so suspiciously."

"No matter what Emily thought your motives were, she'd still have objected to anything that wasn't blue." Janet sighed. "You were bound to start something with her no matter what you did, near as I can tell."

"Nice save—I owe you." He whistled through his teeth. "Man, I didn't realize I'd need a Sherpa in Kentucky."

"A what?"

"A Sherpa. You know, those wise, knowledgeable guides who keep people from killing themselves as they try to climb Mount Everest?"

"Well, this is Middleburg. I think even highly trained professionals couldn't help but step on a few toes here. You've done pretty good so far."

He turned to her and smiled.

"Would you really do that?" Drew asked. "Look over the plans and help me make sure Howard and Emily and anybody else doesn't get upset? The stress level's only going to go up around here as it is as we get closer to deadline. I'd like to avoid all the conflict I can."

It was a sensible request. And she was the closest thing Drew had to an impartial advisor.

"I've got a bunch of site meetings this afternoon and an early dinner at Howard's. Can I bring them by later, like six-thirty?"

Janet hesitated. The store would be closed, which would mean he'd need to bring them by her house. She wasn't sure she was ready for that. Still, she was a twenty-eight-year-old woman. It wasn't like she needed a hall pass to have a man stop by her house for perfectly respectable reasons. She could even show him the birdhouses.

He must have sensed her hesitation, for he added, "I can only stay an hour anyway—we've got the prayer meeting at eight. We can meet somewhere else if you'd feel better about it. Or put it off until morning."

You're being ridiculous, Janet told herself. It's an hour to go over plans, not a romantic rendezvous. Besides, if you meet him on the bus there'll be no way you can escape staying for the prayer meeting. "Come on by. Two blocks over, one block down. 82 Anthem Lane."

Drew looked at her. "Ballad, March, Anthem, you people do like your music-inspired street names."

"You're on to our little secret. There's even a Lullaby Lane, but nobody can stomach the address enough to live on it."

Drew shook his head. "Then why don't you just change the…?" He thought better of his suggestion in light of recent events. "Yeah, right, not really a change-friendly town, are we?"

Janet tucked her hands into her pockets. "Now you're catching on, Downing. Even if it's foolish, chances are we'll keep it around rather than risk something new."

Checking his watch, Drew turned to go. "Man, you'd better go over those plans with a microscope if I'm to get out of this alive," he called back as he headed toward the door. "Six-thirty, 82 Anthem Lane."

Chapter Eleven

Drew didn't know what he'd expected Janet's house to look like, but it surprised him nonetheless. It was a practical little brick house, basic yet with small-town charm. She'd changed out of the overalls and into a pair of soft mauve corduroy pants and a thickly knit cream turtleneck. It changed her features—all that texture in those hues. Gave her a sensible softness, a girl-next-door femininity that caught him unawares.

She showed him to the dining room, where she'd cleared off the large table so he could spread out his plans, swatch books and color palettes he and the design team had pulled together. The table was nearly completely covered once he spread everything out.

"Jeremy's trying to stay within a botanical palette—nature-inspired colors but bright enough to engage little eyes." He pointed to a drawing of some shelving. "We took the motif from the crown molding in the sanctuary and used it here. It'll mean custom work, but I think it'll be worth it."

"You don't need to custom cut that. Look at the shelves my dad built in the library. It does something like that, but we were able to use some stock molding on the straight pieces and only had to do the corner blocks as custom work."

Drew tried to remember what he'd seen in the library. "We won't find that molding in stock anywhere. I've never seen it before."

Janet reached for the pencil and began sketching on a blank space of the paper. "Well, not exactly, but if you take a piece like this—" she sketched out one set of angles "—and combine it with a piece like this—" she sketched out a second set "—all you have to do is cut down this one part here and they'll fit together to make ones really close to the moldings in the sanctuary." She fiddled with the sketch again until, sure enough, the two shapes came together in something amazingly close to the custom design he'd proposed. Her solution cut their costs in half, not to mention the labor-hours needed to install the shelves. He watched her stand up, cock her head from side to side as she analyzed the drawing, then lean back over and make a tiny revision. She had long, delicate fingers, and she held her pencil with the precise grip of an artist.

"That'll work," he said, genuinely impressed. "I mean, that'll *really* work. Half the cost and one-third the time. You know your stuff."

She grinned at him, silently accepting the compliment before pointing to another place on the plans. "Where'd this design come from?"

"Isn't it great? I picked it up from the communion table."

Janet shook her head. "Nope, you can't."

Drew raised an eyebrow. "Preservation?"

"Well, I think this more qualifies as good old Southern orneriness. Old man Nichols made that table, and according to my mama, he'll think you're copying him and pitch a fit for years to come." She stuck her pencil behind her ear. "He has an Olympic medal in fit-pitching, so everyone knows to steer clear. It looks neat, but it's not worth the battle."

"Rats. I liked that one."

"If it makes you feel any better, I do, too."

She'd paid him a compliment again. It didn't sound so foreign in her voice this time, either. Janet Bishop was coming around. Slowly, inch by inch, but some part of him liked that. It meant she was thinking things through, that he was earning her allegiance, not just charming it out of her.

By the end of the conversation, they'd actually laughed together often, their eyes holding for short bits of time. She really did have astounding eyes. The cream sweater she wore made them all the more dark and rich and mesmerizing. He found himself stopping for moments in midsentence, frozen by her eyes. He'd lost his train of thought more than once, bringing them to absurd pauses and flustered excuses. She smelled clean and flowery, like fine soap or a summer breeze. When she reached back up into her hair for the pencil and he noticed the tiny dangle earrings she wore, he'd almost knocked over his drink. She was beautiful. Not pretty—that was too flimsy a word—she was from the inside out beautiful.

"Come back to the bus with me," he said softly. It was as if it crept out of his mouth without his permission.

Janet straightened instantly, giving him a harsh look. Every inch of the guard she'd finally let down shot back up twice as thick as before. "Said the spider to the fly," she quoted in a bitter tone.

What? It took Drew a minute before he realized what he'd said and how she took it. He'd stuck his foot in his mouth—again, only worse. "No! Wait, I didn't mean it that way—what's the matter with me lately? I meant come back to the *meeting* tonight."

Her look told Drew that question didn't meet with

any better reception. "Don't do that," she snapped, actually backing away a few steps from him.

"Do what?"

"Don't make this about faith."

The ice in her words told him just how much of a misstep he'd made. This couldn't even be qualified as resistance, this was blatant refusal. He'd struck a very raw nerve. Drew backed off to sit down on one of the chairs lined up on the side of her dining room. "But I can't make this not be about faith—at least for me. It's all about faith. You know what *Missionnovation* is all about. Your mom's been a prayer warrior for us since the day we pulled in. Dinah goes to that church. Emily and Gil go to that church. Howard and your mother and even Vern go to that church. How can you be all around this church like you are, but not in it?"

"I don't know that it's any of your business. I'm not 'in it.' People around here have learned to respect that, I'd appreciate it if you did, too."

"I can. I respect it." And he did, to a point. The mystery of why Janet was surrounded by people of faith but was so resistant to faith herself was driving him crazy. It seemed too personal to ask anyone but Janet herself, but he'd hoped to be more sensitive about it than this. "I…I just mostly want to understand." Great job, Downing, he yelled at himself. Way to stick your foot in it again. She began rolling up the drawings. He was being dismissed, and his impulsive can't-leave-it-alone nature had shot yet another opportunity in the foot by moving too fast. When would he ever learn?

"No, you don't want to understand. You want to bring me back into the fold. Redeem me. Help me get over my resistance."

It stung him that she'd used the very word in his thoughts. Had he been that transparent?

"How many times do you think I hear lines like that? With my mom pushing that agenda on me daily, you think I can't see it coming a mile off?" She handed him the rolled up drawings and began piling up the swatch books. "You think I wasn't just waiting for it? Congratulations, Drew, you actually took longer than most people. I suppose I should give you credit for that."

"No, Janet, don't. It's not like that. I'm not trying to…" She glared at him, those brown eyes burning, and he knew that was a lie. "Okay, I'm always trying to…but…" He'd botched this, and he knew it. She looked colder than ever, all the softness and texture swallowed by icy defensiveness. He picked up the swatch books off the table. "Nobody wants Jesus stuffed down their throats. But believe me, that wasn't what I meant to do. It was impulse. I'm sorry I offended you. Don't blame God for my stupid behavior." Drew didn't even look up. "I'm going. Good night. I'm sorry." Muttering recriminations to himself, he piled his arms full of everything he'd brought and pushed out the door as fast as he could.

He was a fool. An impatient, insensitive, egotistical clod.

Janet stared at her closed door, fuming. She was mad for eleven different reasons, half of which didn't make sense. She knew better than to think faith wouldn't come up in this. She'd known from before he parked in front of her hardware store that he was all about the God thing. No one was forcing her to be involved beyond filling supply orders. No one was even forcing her to be the job supplier, for that matter (except maybe her balance sheet, but that was hardly God's territory). Downing was as nonstop God as her mother…as Tony. She'd known that all along. She'd already seen that Drew's job and life and faith were inseparable—this shouldn't have surprised her.

He'd been abrupt, but when wasn't he? He'd been bold, but he was bold about everything. And why had she jumped to the conclusion she did when he asked? Why had she assumed he was hitting on her?

The answer made her more prickly than before: because she liked him. She found him attractive in a way that seemed dangerous and unattainable. Irrational, even. He was the opposite of her practicality—a wild, ignore-the-odds loose cannon of a guy who believed he couldn't out-dare God. Tony had been like that, and it still looked enthralling to her—to live on the edge of faith like that. It wasn't something she could ever attain now, though. She couldn't make those kinds of leaps of faith anymore.

Why couldn't Drew Downing have been a different kind of thrill seeker? A race car driver or a test pilot? Why wouldn't God leave her alone like she asked?

Chapter Twelve

Drew stomped into the bus, threw his designs down onto the desk and yanked open the fridge to grab a bottle of water. He didn't open the bottle, but paced across the bus floor, fighting the urge to sock himself between the eyes.

"Whoa, buddy." Kevin came out from the back bunks, looking barely awake. "Take it down a notch or you'll break the bus." He ran his hands through his hair and looked at Drew. "What's going on?"

"Me. I'm going on. I'm saying stupid things and insulting people." Drew began to tear at the *Missionnovation* label, shredding it off the bottle in tiny frustrated pieces. "I'm an impulsive idiot, Cooper. I can't keep up."

Kevin yawned and leaned against the cabinets. "Well, what do you know? Mr. Unstoppable found the end of his rope. Welcome to the world of mere mortals. It only took you three seasons to get here."

"Way to encourage, Kevin. Who knew you had a gift for it?"

Kevin sat down. "No, really. The trouble is you're so busy vaulting over walls you forget what it feels like to hit up against one. You hit a snag—okay, maybe a big snag. It doesn't mean *Missionnovation*'s coming down around your ankles." He reached back behind him toward the coffeemaker. "Grab the plans and we'll see what we can work out."

"This isn't a plan snag. It's a people snag."

"Okay, this town's a bit of a handful, and I heard all about the door business, but this isn't anything you haven't dealt with before."

Drew let his head fall into his hands. "It's a *person* snag. Singular."

Kevin only grunted as he plucked a mug off the back wall and filled it with coffee.

Might as well out with it. "Female."

"Oh." Kevin drew out the word. "Well, what do you know? You and Annie finally…"

Drew shot upright. "Annie? What are you talking about?"

"Hey, I always just figured it was a matter of time before you and Annie…you know."

Drew blinked and looked at his friend. "Annie?

Me and Annie? Are you crazy? Work ethics aside, she's like my kid sister, Cooper. That's just…"

Kevin shook his head. "No, man, she's *not.*"

There was just way too much subtext in Kevin's voice to even contemplate the details. "Cooper…"

Kevin held up his hands in defense. "Hey, I'm just saying behind those glasses…"

"Man, when you jump to conclusions, you really jump to conclusions." He looked at Kevin again, completely stunned. *"Annie?"*

"Okay, so it's not Annie. Pretty clear on that. So if it's not Annie, who is it?"

All of a sudden Drew wasn't sure he wanted to say anything. "Look, forget it. I'll work it out."

Kevin came over and sat on the couch beside Drew. "You came in here stomping mad. You don't normally get like that. If something really got to you, let me help. I'm brilliant, remember?"

Now didn't seem like the best time for true confessions. Drew just eyed his friend. He was still reeling from being linked up with Annie. "Your humility is underwhelming."

"C'mon, Drew, who's getting to you?"

Drew pressed his fingers to his temples. Suddenly he felt exhausted. "Janet Bishop."

That was obviously not the answer Kevin was expecting. "Bishop? The hardware lady?"

Drew nodded. It had made him crazy the whole

walk back to the bus—it seemed even worse to admit it out loud. "The hardware lady."

"Buddy." Kevin shook his head slowly. "That's a bad idea. On all levels."

"I know."

"This is work, Drew. Getting involved would only hurt you and a load of other people."

"I *know*."

"Even if it weren't work, she's got a wall five miles high and two miles thick."

"Tell me about it. I just hit that wall head-on about an hour ago."

Kevin gave a low whistle before taking another swig of coffee. "And you know, Drew, maybe that's the trouble right there. You're the kind of guy who gets way too much fun out of tearing down walls. Don't do it. Nothing good can come out of it. It'll only mess things up. Bad."

Drew glared at Kevin. "Don't you think I know that? On—as you put it—'all levels'?" He fell back against the couch cushions. "What do I do?"

"Pray hard and do your job," Kevin said, refilling his coffee cup. "Pray for the focus to do the job you were sent to do. A few weeks and you'll be out of here, with Middleburg behind you and the season wrapped up and done. You're tired. You picked a big project, you wanted to go out with a bang, and the workload's just getting to you."

"Yeah, sure," Drew said with his eyes closed, the words sounding as hollow as they felt. "I'm just confused, and I guess I've been letting the workload put the squeeze on my prayer time. I've been making mistakes this week I never usually make."

"You've been running full tilt for five months. It caught up with you, that's all. Look, I know there were days when it was just you and Charlie and a whole lot of energy. You've done amazing things. God's done amazing things through you. And, man, we're all thrilled to be part of this. So hang on, buddy, we've got your back. You don't have to hold this up all by your lonesome. Just refocus and get some of that prayer time back, and you'll be okay. We'll be okay."

"You're right." Drew actually yawned.

Kevin pulled one of the travel mugs out of the cabinet and dumped his coffee into it. "Tell you what—it's almost an hour until the prayer meeting. I'll clear out of here and go help Annie with the flyers outside. You put your feet up. Catch a chat with the Guy Upstairs. Then take a nap. I'll come back and wake you before the meeting." With that, Kevin pushed on Drew's shoulders until he slumped down on the couch. "Welcome to the human race, Mr. Hardware Hero. We all gotta crack sometime. But it'll be fine."

* * *

Drew looked out the bus windows at the dawn coming up over the mountains. Sunrises were a lush, misty spectacle in this part of the country. The sun cast a stunning palate of colors as it eased its way over the rolling hills. A dozen different tones of orange and yellow, an array of silver fog and green shadow that melted as the day invaded over the treetops. You could paint the thing a million times and still not capture the quiet marvel of it all. How easy it was to see God the Creator in all the natural beauty here.

Last night's prayer meeting had been great. Solid and inspiring—drawing a larger crowd each night. To Drew, however, his participation still felt hollow. Rote. He couldn't shake the notion that he'd added nothing—that they could have done the meeting without him.

Maybe God was trying to tell him something.

He looked at Charlie's fax and thought maybe it was his place to fly out of here and attend that meeting. Perhaps Charlie was right—he didn't need to be as hands-on as he had in the previous seasons. He'd found great people and formed them into an incredible team. What if God really was calling him to be running out ahead of that team, being the visionary, clearing the way for the others instead of working beside them? What if it really was his own

ego—not his integrity—holding him to the job site?
The illusion of his indispensability?

Maybe he should leave. It surely couldn't hurt
to clear his head and get out of Middleburg for a
day. Twenty-four hours made it a good test for the
team to take the reins. To strengthen their skills
and sense of teamwork for the seasons ahead.

He picked up a Muffinnovation and peeled off
the paper before downing it as breakfast. He ought
to take an order of these to the meeting as a treat.
A little down-home goodie for all those slick
producer types.

Charlie was right. If Hollywood wouldn't come
to Kentucky, then he'd bring Kentucky to Hollywood—*Missionnovation* style. He licked the
green glaze off his fingers before punching
Charlie's speed dial into his cell phone.

"But you *never* leave a site." Annie stared at
him, more surprised than the rest of the team even
though she'd been the one to hand Drew the fax
earlier in the week. "In three seasons I've never
seen you leave a site—not once. I thought it was
a rule of yours."

"It was," Drew explained as he met with the
team that afternoon to outline his upcoming
schedule. "And it was a good policy then. But I've
got you guys now, and I trust you with anything.

This meeting could be taking us to a new level of sponsorship next season. I've prayed about this and I think God's calling me to take on some new roles. Meetings and stuff. Charlie's worked wonders out there on the coast and it's time for me to step in and secure *Missionnovation*'s future."

"I know I said we had your back, but *now?*" Kevin narrowed his eyes. "It can't wait two weeks until we're done here? I mean, we're not that big a deal that it can't wait two weeks."

Drew shrugged his shoulders. "Charlie says now. I trust Charlie to know his job as much as I trust you guys to know yours. He said now because now is when it has to be. You know these network types—they think the whole world revolves around them and they're used to getting what they want. So, I've got to humor them, and if it works out, we'll have twice the budget and twice the outreach we've had before."

Annie looked skeptical, drumming her fingers against her coffee mug. "Humoring? This isn't your style, Drew."

"I admit I wasn't a fan of the idea. And I know Charlie's tried a dozen alternatives. But this is what we've got to work with. I think maybe God's telling me it's time I was less hands-on."

"You don't know how to do 'less hands-on.'"

Mike hardly ever said anything, so this qualified as an outburst from him.

"Oh, this is out of the box for me, no doubt about it. Don't think I'm not walking in faith on this one. But God's called us to new territory before, and He hasn't let us down yet." Drew looked around the bus, catching each team member's eyes. "I've thought long and hard about this. It's not that big a deal—we're getting bogged down in the principle and forgetting the logistics. It's only twenty-four hours. God's big enough to hold us up for one measly Tuesday. Possibly one very beneficial, very future-expanding Tuesday."

"Well," said Annie, blowing out a breath and opening her notebook to what Drew guessed was next Tuesday's production schedule, "I suppose you may have a point. It is only one day."

Annie's approval was enough to get the rest of the team on board—and Drew knew that would be the case. Annie knew how everything worked together to make *Missionnovation* happen. Kevin might have sensed a warm, mutual respect between them, but he was pretty sure it didn't extend beyond the professional. Kevin's remark still baffled him. He needed Annie, but not in the way Kevin thought. If Annie decided they could survive without Drew on-site, everyone else would follow her lead.

He was far less clear about the subject of Janet

Bishop, however. The only thing he knew for sure was that he had to set things right with her before he took one step out of Middleburg.

Chapter Thirteen

Drew found Janet sitting on the floor at the back of the cleaning products aisle, pricing a case of spray bottles with a marker. He loved that about this place. The store was cluttered, but in an organized, "got everything you'll ever need" kind of way. It had character and individuality. Narrow aisles lined with wooden bins and a real counter, not a check-out aisle. No bar codes, no price tags—everything had a price written on it by hand. By her, he guessed, for every product was priced with the neatly drawn numbers one generally attributes to artists or engineers. A sharp but decidedly feminine script.

He tucked his hands in his pockets and stood there until she looked up from her task. He didn't know what to make of her expression. It was softer than the glare she'd given him when he first arrived in Middleburg, but it was far harder than the looks she'd given him over pie at Deacon's Grill. "Hey," he said, oddly tongue-tied for a further greeting.

"'Afternoon," she said, picking up another spray can. "Your blue paint came in. I had Emily look it over just as a precaution."

All business. He supposed he deserved no less. "Thanks for that."

She priced the can and picked up another without looking up. Drew moved over and sat down a foot or two away from her. "Look, I messed up. I knew better than to push like that. That's not the way God is supposed to work, and it's my fault, not His. *Missionnovation* invades enough as it is— it's not supposed to be shoved personally down your throat like that. I'm asking you to forgive my thoughtlessness and let us start over for the sake of the preschool. Can we do that?"

Her pen stilled but she didn't look up. He waited, saying a prayer that God could cover his dumb mistake and make things right between them. He needed Janet's cooperation if this thing was going to come off well. He needed Janet's forgiveness for a whole other bunch of reasons.

"Yes," she said, finally looking up. Her eyes were softer now, but still very cautious. "We can do that."

Drew started to say something clever and

charming to cover the moment, but stopped himself. "Thank you," he said simply, and turned to go.

"Drew," she called as he started down the aisle. He turned.

"Vern has your paint up by the counter. Why don't you ask Emily and Gil to come help you paint the door? Might go a long way with those two." She nodded, and the faintest hint of a smile found its way to the corners of her mouth.

"Brilliant idea. I'll do that."

That night, Janet dropped her mother off at the prayer meeting after they'd had dinner together. After the unavoidable "you're sure you won't stay?" pleading, Janet let her mother out of the car and pulled her Jeep up over the hill towards home. Her cell phone slid and fell between the seat, and she had to stop the car to reach down and fetch it back. At that moment, she heard the sounds of the prayer meeting floating out into the night.

She heard Drew's voice as he spoke to the crowd. He was eloquent—as eloquent as Tony had been, if not more. Tony was a gifted speaker, one of those natural-born leaders who could inspire others to follow him. It wasn't hard to see where most of her suspicion of Drew came from; he was far too much like Tony—like Tony in the early days, that is—not to compare the two. Not

being much of the leader type herself, she admired
those gifts. She wasn't blind to how people naturally followed Drew's dynamic lead.

But it was precisely that "natural following"
that made her nervous. She'd "naturally followed"
Tony, and it had led to nothing but pain. She no
longer trusted the tug she felt when she watched
someone give an impassioned speech.

In some way, though, that was the difference
between what Tony did and what Drew was doing.
There was another side to Drew—one she saw
when he apologized this afternoon—that wouldn't
let her dismiss him as yet another "visionary"
church guy stirring up support. She realized, as
she listened, that she'd been so quick to see the
"hype" that she'd dismissed the passion. They
weren't the same thing. She'd expected a flamboyant, energetic speech—something to beget
handclapping and shouting. Instead, she heard
someone was picking on a guitar, lilting and soft.
She realized she'd been envisioning the meetings
as a sort of God-soaked pep rally, but this wasn't
like that at all.

Drew's voice was different than what she saw
on television or even on site. The voice she heard
now was miles away from the frenetic show
host—this voice belonged to the Drew she saw in
the store this afternoon. For some reason, while

she could easily dismiss the theatrical Drew, this quieter Drew made it impossible to drive away.

He began singing a hymn, and she heard the crowd join in. It was an extraordinary sound, to hear so many voices echoing into the fading light. No wonder they never showed these on television. Even from this distance, the meeting sounded too personal, too intimate to broadcast. It felt almost like church, and she was surprised that the sensation didn't cause her to bristle.

This wasn't hype.

This was worship.

Janet allowed herself to listen, just for a minute. Drew's voice sounded hungry for faith. It was hard to think of him hungering for more. He had enough faith for six people.

She'd grown comfortable with a life without faith. Learned to stand on her own in the practical, pragmatic world she made. She was never the kind of woman who pretended to be something other than who she was—never dyed her hair or wore lots of makeup or needed to run off to college far away from Middleburg. She was who she was—always had been.

But they were both lonely.

She knew why he'd invited her, why he'd blurted that request before he could even realize that she wasn't ready for it. He'd felt it.

That thing she felt, that thing she was trying *not* to feel. There was something between them. Something so impractical, that it seemed ridiculous to entertain.

Janet shook her head and drove away. "Not a chance," she told herself in the rearview mirror. "Not even the slightest chance."

Janet meant to stay away from the work site; she wasn't ready to see Drew again. Theoretically, he was still the same man, but the sides of him she'd seen wouldn't mesh in her head no matter what she tried, and it seemed better just to stay away.

Vern, however, had gone to the prayer meeting for the first time last night and wouldn't stop talking about it. "No hoopla there," he said as he and Janet opened the store that morning. "Just fine, upstandin' hymn singin'. Like the revivals we had when I was young." Janet heard him mutter "good people" three or four more times before she couldn't stand it anymore.

"Run this over to the church, will you?" she interrupted, handing Vern a tin of drywall compound. "Ask somebody if this is the kind they want." Of course, no one had even ordered drywall compound. The outer walls were just barely up. Still, if she didn't get Vern and his green-bus-gushing out of here she was sure she'd go bananas. "We're more than covered for the morning," Janet lied, "why don't you have some fun and hang around the site for a few hours. Let me know what you think of the way they've run the utilities over there."

He jumped at the invitation. She knew he would. Besides, a morning alone in the shop seemed like just the tonic for her frazzled insides.

Drew looked at Vern and Mike as the pair of them hauled some equipment across the lawn. Side by side like that, Vern and Mike looked like father and son. Like Mike—*Missionnovation*'s long and lanky electrics expert whom punsters often called "wiry"—Vern hadn't a pound to spare on his tall frame. They'd obviously hit it off; they were absorbed in an animated conversation. This was half the fun of *Missionnovation*—watching folks make friendships. Drew himself kept up regular correspondence with several people from projects from each of the seasons—it had become an extended family of sorts for him. Despite the doubtful eye Vern had given the bus when it first pulled up, Drew liked the guy. They'd talked several times over the past few days. The old man had asked pointed questions, but he also seemed satisfied with the answers Drew provided. He was a straight shooter all right, honest but fair, and he had the wisdom of age Drew missed with his father now gone.

They were debating some technical point when Drew caught up with them. "Have you met Vern here?" Mike said, putting down the wheelbarrow he was pushing.

"I most certainly have," Drew pulled off his work glove and shook Vern's hand again. Vern had come over just after nine, and it was well past noon, but still the man showed no signs of wanting to either go home or get back to Bishop Hardware. "Good to have your help, sir."

"Your man knows his way around his pipes and wires," Vern said, inclining his head toward Mike. "It's been a long time since someone showed me something I didn't already know."

Mike beamed. He really was an expert with electrics and plumbing, but the general public wasn't always appreciative of the wonders behind their walls. Mike always grumbled, "People don't give a hoot about their wiring until it stops working. Then all they do is hoot and holler." It was true.

"I was just showing him how we rigged the upstairs conduit boxes," Mike started in. "He liked how we…"

Drew held up his hand before Mike launched into something highly technical. "I trust you with the details. And believe me, if Vern's impressed, then I am, too."

Vern looked at Drew with a narrowed eye. "You know what you got in this guy? How good he is?"

Drew had to smile. It was grand that Mike found someone who truly appreciated his skills. Especially someone as frugal with their praise as Vern Murphy. "I do indeed, sir."

"Well, you make sure you remember that. Fine young man. I reckon a hotshot like you would be sunk without the likes of him."

Drew clasped a hand onto Mike's shoulder. "I thank God every day for Mike." And he did. Drew could design anything a church wanted, but if the lights and plumbing didn't work, *Missionnovation* might as well be handing out tents and boxes.

"Vern agrees with my changes to the hallway lighting, you know." Mike and Drew had come to a serious disagreement yesterday over the placement of some lights in the preschool wing.

Vern crossed his arms over his chest and gave Drew a pointed look. He knew that look—he'd seen it on half a dozen former hostiles. It was the look that said "I'm going to base my opinion of *Missionnovation* on what you say next."

Drew's gaze shifted from Mike's defiant look to Vern's challenging stare. Hadn't his father had always taught him that sometimes you need to give to get? Drew was smart enough to see he was currently outnumbered. "So Vern thinks we ought to do it your way, does he?"

"Yep." Mike's arms came up to cross his chest until he looked like Vern's younger mirror image.

Definitely outnumbered. "Well, then, I concede to Mr. Murphy's wise counsel." Mike's and Vern's twin grins only exaggerated their similarities. Drew was just thinking about what an education in life this job was when he spied Janet coming across the lawn.

She stopped, put her hands above her eyes against the bright sunshine, and scanned the site.

"Vern," Drew said as he caught Janet's expression, "Did you play hooky this morning, sir?"

"What do you mean by that?" Vern came up behind him.

Drew pointed to Janet, scanning the site with a hand impatiently planted on one hip. "I think Ms. Bishop's wondering where you've gone off to."

Vern gave a low whistle. "Well of course she knows I'm here. She sent me. Told me to stay awhile besides."

Drew gave Vern a look. "Maybe 'awhile' didn't mean close to four hours. I'm obliged, Vern, but don't lose your job over us."

Vern nudged Mike. "She cain't fire me. I got seniority."

"Vern," Drew replied, "I reckon you got more seniority than any of us. But even young upstarts like me know you've got to keep the boss happy."

"Yeah, well if you'd seen her this mornin' you'd know nothin' was gonna keep her happy today," Vern said. Then he turned to Mike. "Between you and me, I was glad to get out of there this morning."

Lord, what is it about that woman? Drew prayed as he put down the cables he was holding and began walking with the old man down the hill.

"It's nearly one," Janet said as Vern came walking across the lawn with Drew. He looked like he'd had a grand time, and she hated herself for coming over to fetch him back like some kind of disciplinarian. "I know I said 'awhile,' but…"

"Thanks for loaning us Vern." Drew interrupted. Those two looked in cahoots with each other. She didn't cherish the idea of Vern siding up with Drew Downing. Then again, there weren't even supposed to be "sides," were there?

"You should see some of the gizmos they got here," Vern said, pulling a red bandana out of his overalls pocket and wiping his brow. Probably fishing for sympathy that he'd been over-worked, Janet decided. "Must be how they get it done so fast."

"And good help," Drew said, shaking Vern's

hand. Janet wondered if the bandana Vern pulled from his pockets wouldn't be *Missionnovation* green tomorrow. She was starting to dislike green.

"Would you mind terribly if Vern came back to work now?" she asked Drew but kept her eyes on Vern. "We need that good help back at the store if I'm to get to the bank this afternoon."

"You can have Vern back, if I can borrow you for a moment. The rest of the gutter work arrived, and I've a question or two about it. You're my expert."

Janet sighed. Wasn't the whole point of this morning to avoid Drew Downing and the *Missionnovation* madness?

"I'll head on back to mind the store," Vern said, and she thought she saw him wink at Drew. "Go on and take your time with that."

Roofs gutters—not exactly foreign territory, Janet thought to herself as she dismissed the looks that passed between Vern and Drew. It had clearly been a mistake to put those two together.

Chapter Fourteen

Drew led her past the collection of tented work-spaces that had sprung up around the church. "The garden's going to be fabulous. I found a stonemason on the other side of town who's going to help us build the terrace here. And he led me to a guy in the area who'll make a gorgeous wrought-iron gate for the garden at half his normal cost. There's a woman from Lexington who's coming out to paint murals on the preschool wall, too. And I was talking to Pastor Anderson the other day, and he's thinking about recommending the full-scale rainwater collection system to other churches." His eyes lit up, as if connecting these people to the project was the most exciting part of his job. "You all have been hit with some bad droughts in recent years, and he thinks this is great stuff we're doing."

Janet stared at Drew. Pastor Anderson was

thinking about recommending the system? The system she couldn't get him to even look at for months back then? You've got to be kidding, she griped to herself, I try for months and he swoops in and gets them on board in a matter of days? "He's that gung-ho, hmm?" She tried to keep the edge of annoyance out of her voice.

Evidently not very well, for Drew's expression softened and he admitted, "Well, he did say he remembered hearing something about the subject 'from Bebe's daughter.' And the prospect of a new roof for the whole church sort of sweetened the deal, I think."

"That, and the state funds."

"Hey, God uses whatever means at His disposal. And we always find what we need. As a matter of fact, most times we find more than what we need."

"Meaning?"

"Meaning that people are generally good." He led her around a corner. "They're usually eager to help, just waiting for someone to ask them. And then they catch the excitement and pass it on to someone else, like the garden gate. That's the real amazing part of *Missionnovation* for me. Not the television part, the connecting part." He spread his hands in illustration. "The ripples that go out from one connection to another. The way people join together."

They had to stop their progress for a second to

let a television camera go by. She chose that moment to say what she'd been biting back for days. "Look, I know you believe that, and I understand what you're saying, but don't you think the television exposure has more to do with it than anything else?" He scowled, and she wondered if she'd been too direct. "Not that it's bad, I suppose, because the work gets done when it might not get done otherwise, but—" she tried to think of a gentle way to put it, but this kind of diplomacy was never her strength "—don't you wonder if you're just kidding yourself about people's motives here?" There, she'd said it.

He stared for a second, and she couldn't tell if he was taken aback or just being very careful about his reply. "Just for the record, I like that about you."

"What?"

"You say what you mean."

Janet looked down. "Well, not everyone sees it as the virtue you do."

He pivoted to stand in front of her. "I've got loads of people telling me what they think I want to hear. I'm aware of what people think of me, of what they think I can do *for* them. Truth is a valuable thing in my world, Janet. I don't always get as much of it as I'd like. So please don't ever be afraid to tell me what you really think. I mean it."

She nodded, unable to come up with another reply.

"Besides," he said, putting his hands in his pockets and walking on again, "since when is holding up the good in people bad? With all the stuff on television these days, what's so bad about showing off what's good and friendly and still right in the world?"

"There's a difference between honest generosity and...I don't know what you'd call it... product placement?"

"Yes, there is." He looked at her over one shoulder. "And while I admit to a bit of an expertise in the area, most people can see the difference. That's part of what I do. That's part of my job— to keep *Missionnovation* on the right path, to watch for that kind of thing and keep it at bay."

"So you admit it happens."

"It does happen. I've rejected offers of help. Things we have no business taking because those people aren't really here to help, but only for exposure. That's one of the reasons I like going out into the community and asking. That's where you find the honest folks. The people just looking to help other people? They're so easy to find, Janet."

Janet wasn't sure she agreed with that remark. She thought about all the people Tony had fooled. She almost told Drew the story, suddenly not wanting him to think her a cynical old spinster, but couldn't reveal something so personal—especially here, with all those annoying cameras around every corner. She settled for shrugging her shoulders, saying, "That's a lot of optimism."

"Maybe, but that's how I've always seen the world." He swung his hand around the work site. "All this isn't that much different than when I was just building houses with charity development organizations. I do it on a larger scale now, and more people know about it."

"Yeah, just a few million."

He looked at her, intensely this time. "It was the same when it was three. Or twelve. Or two hundred. Honestly, it might have even been more fun."

They wound their way around the back to where the little preschool garden sat nestled into the hillside. The benches—artfully curved and tot-sized—were still unpainted and piled up on one side. The motor works for the fountain was still above ground, and the fishpond was upside down on the ground without its hole dug yet. Even so, she could clearly see the finished product in her head. It was darling. She couldn't help but smile.

"See," Drew said, nudging her with a grin on his face. "That's something else I like about you. Other people look at this and they see a chaotic construction site. You look at this and you see the outcome. Check this out." He walked over to where the cistern stood. "We're gonna build a housing around this to make it look like a giant watering can."

Wasn't that a bit much? Water tanks were fine just as they were; they didn't need to look like they came from a theme park.

Drew caught her scowl and held up his hand. "No, no really, it's brilliant when you think about it. Right now, all they know is that God made it storm and their preschool went away. Now, they'll see how God waters the earth." He made an oversize watering gesture next to the cistern. "Can't you just see God's mighty hand picking up this giant watering can to make their little garden grow?"

"The system works on gravity. I'm pretty sure it's got to be underground to work best."

"You can do them both ways. This way's gonna be fabulous. So many people are already lending their hand to make it great. But it's missing one thing. It's missing your birdhouses. You haven't said yes, yet." He stared into her eyes as if her answer were the hinge pin to the entire project's success. It did something to her, pulled up something from deep inside. She hesitated.

"Say yes." His voice softened to the quiet tones she'd heard in the dusk yesterday.

She knew, right then, that it would be impossible not to say yes. It was bubbling up from somewhere under her ribs even now.

"Will you? Please?" He winced. "I don't want to build this garden without those birdhouses. I want your art to be part of the community that makes this garden."

She shifted her weight back onto one hip. "I need to think about it."

"Well, I suppose I can't ask for more than that." He picked up one of the fence posts lying on the ground and inspected it. "I'm not famous for my patience, but I can wait until I get back."

Janet sat on a stack of fencing. "Get back?"

Drew sighed. "I've got to leave on Tuesday and go to a big network meeting about the next season. Glad-hand sponsors, pitch our cause, that sort of thing."

"You're leaving?"

"Just for a day. They insisted I be there." He sat down near her on the pile of fencing slats. "I'm not happy about it, but there doesn't seem to be any other way."

"You're the boss. Who's ordering you around?" Janet tucked one leg underneath her. "I hardly think God himself called you to head on up to L.A. and make nice with the sponsors."

Drew chuckled. "Charlie'd laugh at that. Charlie Buchanan, our executive producer. I'm the build man, he's the biz man. I trust him, but I've never left a site before in all three seasons of *Missionnovation.*" He leaned a fraction of an inch closer to her. "You, you really are the boss. Me, I just play one on TV."

"So now you're saying you don't like what you do?" It seemed a ridiculous question given his exuberance.

"I love what I do. I just don't always love how I have to do it." He picked up the post again and thumped it on the ground in front of him, as if testing how it would look upright. "What about you? Do you love what you do?"

As the only offspring of Ronald and Bebe Bishop, it had been a given from her first breath that she'd work in the store. Loving that never came into the equation. As such, her first impulse was to say the expected thing, something easy like "Sure I do," but she choked on the words.

"It…needed doing."

"What if it didn't?" He looked at her. "What would you love to do? Would you build amazing little birdhouses all day?"

She wondered if anyone even remembered her college major. "No. I'd build amazing big houses. For people." It felt like someone else was answering for her, some daring other Janet he'd managed to tug out of her with his eyes.

"Architect?"

"I have half a degree. Three quarters of one, actually. I always meant to go back and finish that last year after we got things settled at the store." That degree felt like an exercise in futility anyway—a stretching of wings that she'd never really get to use. It hadn't even really been a decision to come home from college when her dad had gotten sick. It had already been decided that she would run Bishop Hardware, and who needed an architect's degree to do that?

A breeze picked up in the trees, showering amber-colored leaves down around them. One fell onto the post, and Drew brushed it off before he thumped the wood on the ground again, turning it to a new angle. "You quit school to come back and help your mom when your dad died?"

"She needed it. She doesn't have it in her to run the store." She picked up one of the leaves that had fallen on the fencing. She held it up to the light, the deep yellow glowing in the low afternoon sun, and spun it around in her fingers. It was wet on one side from the brief rain shower that had come overnight. "And you know Vern would curl up and die if he didn't have Bishop Hardware." She tried to make it sound like a joke, but it came out with a sad little lilt. It made her wonder about the dear old man. Had he thought he'd be the one to run Bishop Hardware after her father died? Why had it never even been discussed? He was as close to being a Bishop as anyone could be without having the actual name.

"Vern." Drew said the name with affection and amazement. "The Verns are all but gone from this world. He's a piece of work, I'll tell you. You don't meet Verns at HomeBase." Somewhere over her shoulder a pair of birds called to each other. She and Drew listened to the exchange for a moment. "No Verns in Los Angeles, either," he continued wistfully. "Nope, the Verns are out here, in the neighborhoods like this one. And they're the most important people, the Verns."

He said it in such an odd way—especially about a man he'd essentially just met. It made her wonder. "You have a Vern in your life, I take it?"

"I did, yeah. Only he was a Hal. A lot like Vern, only younger—and fatter, too." Drew chuckled. "A great big man, as a matter of fact. Could devour barbecue ribs and gospel music like no one I've ever met since." She saw that same distant look, the one that took those intense eyes far back into his memory.

"A pastor or something?"

Drew laughed. "Not at all. Well, maybe in a radical sense of the word. He pastored me, but not in a church pew. I wouldn't have darkened the door of a church in my earlier days. I was a pretty wild guy growing up." He stole a look at her. "I'm sure you can't imagine that, given my personality."

"Well—" she nodded "—you're such the shy type."

"In college I was the wild guy. Full-out, one-hundred-percent intensity in all directions." He spread his hands in front of him. "Including several less-than-healthy ones. I liked to be entertained, enthralled, and I found some pretty daring ways to do it. I'll spare you the sordid details, but let's just say by my sophomore year in college, I was a pretty lost soul in every sense of the word. Film school is a really easy place to explore your dark side."

Film school. That explained his ease with the cameras, Janet supposed. And his tendency to be in front of them. "Believe it or not, it's a rather ordinary story," he began. Janet regretted asking, realizing he'd taken her inquiry as an opening to tell his testimony.

She wasn't sure she wanted to have that kind of a conversation with him—especially here. "I did a documentary on Hal. He was working in Detroit, fixing up houses for poor people. No great organization, no big-time fundraising, just one big guy and his hammer and a whole lot of determination." He pulled a screwdriver from his tool belt and fiddled with it, spinning it absentmindedly between his fingers. "Hal would always keep on, no matter the obstacle. I couldn't understand what kept him running, what kept him striving against these incredible hurdles and people who didn't even seem to thank him for the amazing things he did. I kept trying to capture it on film, but none of the footage explained his persistence. So I asked him one night."

Hadn't Janet wondered something close to that about Drew? How he could keep the insane schedule he kept? Exude the non-stop energy he did? Even though she knew where this would lead, she couldn't help but ask, "What'd he tell you?"

"He just looked at me, as if it was the most obvious thing in the world, and said 'Jesus.' Like that explained everything. But it didn't—at least not for me—so I kept asking him. I knew lots of people who claimed to be religious, but none of them acted the way he did. Most of them were in your face and down your throat. But not Hal—he never even tried to talk to me about it until I came and asked him."

"A mistake *you've* never made," she said, not entirely teasing.

"Yeah, well we've all got our own styles. I happen to think your Vern's a bit of an in-your-face kind of guy, too. He just took Mike's side in an argument we were having, and I had to back down and give in."

"He's like family, Vern. Annoying and wonderful and irreplaceable." She veered the conversation away from Drew's journey to faith. "You can't win an argument with Vern. I half went off to college just to stop his nagging. I brought him back an Ohio State sweatshirt for every year I went."

"But you didn't get to finish." Drew laid the post back on the ground and looked at her. "I think I get it about the birdhouses now. Don't sell them to us if you're not ready. I thought they were just a hobby, but they're more than that. They're bits of a dream, and I wouldn't want you to lose that."

Janet saw him so clearly at that moment. She understood how the high-voltage man and the quieter man co-existed. His motivation—the person-to-person connections that energized him—were just hidden by the show's grand scale. He wasn't a conman. He was just a guy who wanted to build things that made people happy. And he wanted her to join in. As he looked at her, the garden around him took on those simple, be-happy qualities. Emily and Gil's kids might come here someday. Maybe, one day if she got the chance, her own children—Bebe's grandchildren—would play in this garden.

If this wasn't worth clearing out her stock of

birdhouses, what was? It wasn't as if she couldn't make more. She could always make more. Suddenly it seemed silly—selfish even—to have ever thought otherwise. After all, birdhouses don't belong on shelves, they belong outside.

"You're right. I'm not ready to sell you my birdhouses," she said.

He looked away and sighed.

"I'm going to give them to you. All of them. And whatever other ones you need, I'll make."

Drew rubbed his head with a towel and put a belt through the loops of a fresh pair of jeans. He didn't really need a shower—he mostly needed time alone. Needed time to figure out just what it was Janet Bishop was doing to him. Why she, above all the other women he'd ever met, was unnerving him in very dangerous ways.

Granted, he was used to being the one in control. Throughout his life, a number of things—his visibility, his looks, his personality, whatever—had granted him success with women. He'd been a charmer in high school and college, and before he came to faith, he'd made the most of that charm. Not that he'd have called himself a womanizer, but he was less than careful with his affections. Prone to flirting, determined to keep the upper hand in relationships, never lingering too long with any one woman lest things get unduly serious.

God had called a halt to lots of that behavior. God hadn't, however, shown him anyone he wanted to get long-term serious with, either. Drew couldn't complain; while he had loads of admirers now (and a high percentage of them were female), there wasn't much time or energy for anything close to a real relationship.

Is that what he wanted—a relationship with Janet Bishop? She certainly fascinated him, but he wasn't sure that was the same thing. She had a unique beauty, but he'd been surrounded by all kinds of beauty in film school without the can't-stop-thinking-about-her reaction he was having now.

It wasn't about how Janet looked or how she acted toward him. It was about who she was. Her character. Her resistance. The wounds he was pretty sure she hid under the surface. She was the human embodiment of what drew him to renovation construction in the first place—find the problem, find the damage and shore it up. Make it stronger. Once he'd ditched film school and decided to work in construction, Drew could have made far more money with his design skills by building new homes and offices. And there were many times in his career where it made monetary or logistical sense to tear down all of an old building and start over from the ground up. His true love, though, was tearing back to the beams, gutting something down to its bones and building the same structure back better. When you got right down to it, Drew's love wasn't so much creating as it was repairing.

He'd created something amazing with Charlie, though. Charlie and he had been in film school together—back in the wild days. They'd parted ways when Drew went off to mission construction work. Charlie had called him a lunatic then, but Charlie had eaten his words when they met up four years later at a fund-raiser. God had orchestrated it with a dramatic sense of style—taken each man and pulled him toward faith in different worlds, only to bring the two of them back together when the time was right. They sat up one night in an all-night diner, talking about how faith and the media seemed at odds, and hit on the basic concept that became *Missionnovation*. They felt like they'd set fire to the world that night—the concept was so strong and so perfectly suited to each of their talents. Drew began doing what he did so well—bringing one person at a time into the idea and letting it expand from the enthusiasm. Charlie began doing what he did best—gathering resources, managing logistics, backing Drew up behind the scenes. The two of them rode God's calling as far as it would take them and hadn't stopped since.

While many people had offered "spin-offs" or related projects, Drew was happy just continuing to work on *Missionnovation*. Tweaking it, improving it, repairing it when it went wrong. He still loved to fix things. *Is that why she fascinates me, Lord? Because I can't figure out how to fix her?* That struck Drew as an arrogant thought. It wasn't his job to repair people. *That's Your territory, Lord. I've no business even thinking I can fix whatever it is that's made her so suspicious.*

But I want to. Badly. And that can't be good.

Every time he thought he'd gotten his attraction to her under control, she'd go and do something to unravel him. Show him some beautiful aspect of her personality that she kept so closely hidden. He suspected he'd eventually get her to sell her birdhouses to the project. Maybe give one away. But to give them all, after what he learned about them? That did something to him that reduced his reason to sawdust. When she'd offered the birdhouses, he'd been blindsided by the urge to kiss her.

Kiss her. *Really, did a more dangerous impulse even exist? The problems that would have caused. The tension, the offense. That'd win first prize for stupid and ungentlemanly conduct. Thank you, Lord, that I didn't do it.*

Still, that didn't erase the fact that he wanted to.

Maybe You are saving me from something by hauling me off to L.A. for a day, Lord. I need to get my head on straight before I mess everything up.

Chapter Fifteen

There was a long list of things to be done before Drew left for L.A. and one of the top priorities was convincing Annie and Kevin to lead the prayer meeting while he was gone. Kevin would do it in a heartbeat—there wasn't a shy bone in the man's body. Annie would take some convincing, but he had a hunch there was a gifted speaker hiding behind that clipboard, and now was a prime time to coax her out.

He located her just in time. She and Kevin were launching into an argument at the southwest corner of the church.

"Those species aren't native," Kevin said sharply. "I don't care if it's the hottest new thing in their seed catalogue. You want to be responsible for an invasive species taking over Kentucky?"

Annie planted a hand on her hip. "They're

annuals, Kevin. As in plants that die every winter. We're hardly staging an alien invasion by using Alphco's featured flower." She pulled a thin booklet off her clipboard and held it out toward Kevin. "They'll give us the rest of the plants at half the cost if we do. They'll be dead next year, and if the folks from Middleburg hate them they can plant whatever else they want."

Kevin snatched the catalogue from her. "I used to think *I* could plant whatever *I* want." Rolling up the catalogue, he shoved it in his back pocket as if he were holstering a gun for a cowboy shoot-out.

Drew shook his head. Those two ended up in at least three arguments per project. He stepped into their line of vision and put on a cheery voice. "Hi, kids, having fun yet?"

Kevin gestured wildly at Drew. "Tell me I don't have to fill this churchyard with hideous purple flowers because Alphco Garden Supply thinks they're this year's cool bloom."

Drew slipped his hands in his pockets. "Kevin, no one's going to force purple flowers on you." Kevin crossed his arms smugly over his chest while Annie fumed. "But," Drew continued, "you should at least listen to Annie if she thinks it's worth doing. Annie knows a lot about these kinds of deals. You just might find she's right." Now it was Annie's turn to look smug. Drew gestured toward her. "Annie, why do we want to love purple flowers this year?"

"Because Alphco will give us a killer discount on the rest of our stuff if we do. Because they're annuals." She shot Kevin a dark look. "Because they're not an invasive species. For all I care, we can dig them up out of the flower beds after we film. But even Howard Epson thinks they're lovely and they'll save us so much money we can pay for your giant watering can."

"I like my giant watering can a lot," Drew said to Kevin. "And it would be smart to show the folks in L.A. we know how to treat our sponsors. Can we live with purple flowers to make those things happen?"

"We use *native species,* Drew. You know how important that is to me. Those purple atrocities are not native."

Annie held her hand out and wiggled her fingers, evidently asking Kevin to return the catalogue. When he did, she turned the catalogue over to show Drew the cover. It hosted a photograph of a purple flower that looked about as ordinary as flowers get. Hardly the atrocity Kevin was lambasting. "It is an engineered variety. It's not native to anywhere except some lab in New Jersey."

"All the *more* reason to steer clear," Kevin howled. "Who knows what we'll get?"

"We'll get thousands of dollars off our bill," Annie shot back. Those two could quibble like siblings when they got into it—and boy, they were into it. Drew was suddenly cast as referee, dad, judge and war crimes tribunal all wrapped up into one flannel shirt.

"Okay, you two, we need to solve this. We need to learn how to handle pressure from sponsors and still do the right thing. Next year, this kind of stuff may only get harder, so let's not shoot ourselves in the foot now." Drew pointed at Kevin. "You get twenty-four hours to see if you can dig up any problems with Alphco engineered varieties." He pointed to Annie. "You get Alphco to agree that if the Middleburg folks have any problems with these blooms we can dig 'em up. They may knock a percentage off their discount, but you can handle it."

Kevin and Annie applied dual scowls for half a minute, then relented. "'*So far as it concerns you, be at peace with one another*,'" Drew quoted, pulling their hands together to shake. "Now that we've got that settled, I've got something else to pose to the two of you. I want you two to lead the prayer meeting for the evening while I'm gone."

"What?" The request had the effect Drew intended; they both instantly forgot their previous argument.

"Someone has to take the lead while I'm gone. I think you're both up for it. You're ready."

Annie gulped and pushed up her glasses. "Ready? I don't think so."

"Annie, if you can pray at the microphone the way you pray at staff meetings—which you can, by the way, you just haven't realized it—we're set. I'll ask someone from the church here to back you up and it'll be wonderful."

Annie shook her head.

"No, I think Drew's right. You're ready to lead the prayer. You're just not ready to lead the singing," Kevin teased, his mood suddenly changing. "You can't sing. But pray—you're a champ. You're great at it."

Annie turned pink. "Praying around a table with people you know, that's one thing. But up there, in front of everyone?"

"We don't film those, you know that." Drew put a hand on her shoulder. "It's just you and some people who believe in prayer as much as you do. It's the friendliest crowd there is. And you are ready for it. You've been ready for it for a while, and God just handed you the perfect opportunity. Can you see that?"

Annie backed away a bit. "Look, Kevin's totally up for leading the singing, so why not let him do the whole thing? Or Jeremy. Let Jeremy be host for a night. I'm a sidelines kind of gal, you know that."

Kevin smiled. "You shouldn't be. Drew's right. You'll be great at it. You should do it, Annie. Really."

"Well..." she hesitated.

"If you don't, Drew might really ask Jeremy, and we all know how that would turn out. C'mon, Annie, prayer is definitely your gift. Share it with the world, not just the bus."

Drew leaned up against the church wall. He knew Kevin would like the idea, but Kevin's enthusiasm for Annie surprised him. Maybe his team was even stronger than he thought. He'd always had to be the one to push them into new territory. Now they were growing into a team who could draw at each other's strengths.

Annie shifted her weight and looked at Drew. He smiled back at her, even though she looked as though she might begin chewing on the end of her pen at any moment. She looked at Kevin, and he smiled broadly, even nodded. "You're sure?" she said after a moment.

"Absolutely," Drew said, at the same moment Kevin said "Totally."

"One prayer? And I can write it out beforehand?"

"Only one, and I don't think you need to write it out beforehand. You pray what's in your heart at the staff meetings, and it's always just perfect. Just think of Middleburg as a really big bus."

Janet stood in her workroom and looked at the eight birdhouses that sat on the shelves. They did seem hoarded back here, sequestered away like a hidden neighborhood. Only they weren't a little neighborhood. Birdhouses aren't birdhouses unless birds are living in them, are they? That was the thought that enabled her to change her mind back there in the garden. When she saw Drew so clearly in the role he was born to, it struck her that her birdhouses weren't living the life they were made for: outside, housing birds.

She picked one of her earliest birdhouses, one that was styled after a Baltimore row house. That was the life she thought she'd been born to—finishing her architectural degree while helping Tony run his social service mission on the East Coast. Only that mission—and, when she thought about it, that Tony—never existed. The birdhouse left a footprint on the dusty Bible underneath it. She didn't remember she'd hidden her Bible up here—and hadn't picked up a Bible since that whole fiasco. She stared at the worn leather volume a long time before she touched it.

It felt like it had been waiting for her. Which was foolish—books didn't have emotions. And

yet, as she looked at the birdhouses surrounding
her, they seemed to be waiting as well. Waiting
for the chance to be birdhouses instead of, well,
coping mechanisms. Somehow, constructing
these tiny houses, the exact science of it, the
carefully controlled art of it had been her
survival. That's why they felt so precious to her.
Taking them out in the world would be like
putting her crawl back from the pain on some
kind of display.

Or setting herself free from it.

She'd have to think about that. A lot. But as she
remembered the look on Drew's face when she'd
given him the birdhouses, part of her knew she'd
already decided. As she stared around the shelves,
she could picture them on the posts around the
garden. And they belonged there, in the garden.
Maybe it was time to move a few things around
in her life.

Janet brushed the dust off the Bible, and while
she didn't open it, she moved it to a corner of her
worktable to sit beside her as she opened some
revised orders Mike had dropped off this afternoon.

What she saw made her heart sink.

They'd done it. There, in black and white under
the very ordinary guise of a revised materials
order, *Missionnovation* had cut corners. On the
roof. Probably the most important, lasting reno-

vation Drew was doing, and the thing they hadn't even requested.

Janet sucked in a breath, reeling from the information as physically as if someone had slapped her. They weren't ordering the roof supplies from Bishop Hardware anymore. A hand-scrawled note from Drew said they were going with an exciting new product supplied by HomeBase. One she'd never heard of—and certainly not something from the list of suggested materials from the rainwater system manufacturer. This was wrong. This was everything she didn't trust about *Missionnovation* wrapped up into one convenient substitution. Sponsorship was winning over quality, and Middleburg was going to pay the price.

Not if she could help it. She dashed to her computer and spent an hour looking over every scrap of information she could find on both HomeBase's product and the ones Drew had planned to use in the first place. HomeBase's product was untested. There were no reviews, no data showing how well it aged or what problems had arisen for users after installation. As far as Janet was concerned, Middleburg Community Church didn't have the spare funds to gamble with some jazzy new roof product. They needed a dependable roof they could count on for a long time. And this wasn't it.

She didn't stop to pick up the Bible when it fell off her worktable as she gathered up her papers. She was going to give Drew Downing a piece of her mind right now, whether he wanted to hear it or not.

Chapter Sixteen

She knew something like this would happen. The minute she let her guard down, it would all go wrong. Janet stood outside the bus door with a stack of papers in her hands and a frown. She knocked loudly. Drew's face appeared, then disappeared for a second as he reached back behind him to pulled the lever that opened the doors. "You've got a problem," she said matter-of-factly as she stomped up the stairs to dump the papers on the bus table. She was a big ball of "I told you so" right now and he was going to hear about it. "I thought you told me no cutting corners."

He looked a bit taken aback, as well he should. "And we don't."

"Yes, you did. Mike left the new roof specs with me. I should have suspected something when you switched some of the orders to

HomeBase. You're not putting the right kind of roof in there, Drew." She pointed to the pile of instructions and Internet search printouts she'd brought with her.

He sat down and motioned for her to do the same. Good. At least he looked like he was going to listen. "Look, I'm sorry we couldn't fill that order with you, but there's nothing wrong with that roof. HomeBase made us an offer and we took it."

"But now you're not using the recommended materials. You're using HomeBase's product instead of one of the recommended materials. And your gutters aren't the right size. *And* according to what I read," she began, "the rainwater system still works best with the storage tank *underground.*"

"That's one of the options, yes. And those roofing materials are identical to the recommended ones. Only with faster installation. *Nothing's* been compromised in terms of quality."

"*Your* opinion, maybe." She'd known he was going to say that. It was a faster option, and less expensive, but she had a lot to say regarding whether it was the best.

"The opinion of everyone else on the team. We've used our assets to get you a great deal on great products."

"Great products? Or ones that install faster and get you your pretty watering can for God?" She hadn't meant it to come out quite so sharply, but he was being so casual and roofs were so important.

"That's not fair."

So maybe it wasn't. She'd gotten surprisingly worked up about this. "All right, that was a bit out of line. But Drew, I don't think this roof is going to do the job. It's not the ideal setup. We need *this*." She pointed to a catalogue of roof tiles she thought were a better choice.

"I need the solution that *works,* Janet, not just the ideal setup." He pointed to her choice. "These are top-notch, but their installation is more complicated, they're much more expensive, and face it—they take more time than we've got. A rushed installation with those isn't automatically a better choice than a solid installation with what I've chosen. Both work."

There it was: the crux she knew they'd reach no matter what kind of ideology he spouted. Confining the job to such a strict time frame forced choices that should never need to be made. Created deadlines that didn't have to exist. "This is exactly my point. The only reason we have a deadline is *because of you.* School's already in session and working out okay. Not great, but okay. We have the time to do this right. *You guys* opt for the quick fix because it fits into *your* television time frame."

He glared at her. "You know, you wouldn't even be *getting* a whole new church roof if it weren't for the pull of our 'television time frame.' Our ability to give this gutter and rainwater stuff television exposure *got you* the best roof available for your building. And it got you the grant. You wouldn't have been able to do that on your own— you told me that yourself. Don't you think that's a fair trade-off?"

She'd wondered when he'd play the "you should be grateful we're here" card. "What good is that roof if it leaks in two years? In two months? Even the water tank's wrong. There're three whole pages in there on the dangers of not putting that tank down low enough. But why should you care? You'll be gone. *Long gone.*" The words choked up in her throat.

Drew stood up, fuming. "I read everything," he fired back. "Mike read it. Kevin read it. We spoke four times with the manufacturer. *Four times.* I don't call that rushing on a decision. That roof will not leak because we know what we're doing. And as for that little jab about God's watering can," he went on, putting a sharp edge on the phrase she'd used, close to the edge of his temper. "I'll tell you something you probably haven't even stopped to think about. That artistic casing is more than just making the thing look like 'God's watering can'. It's insulation. A layer of protection against the elements that still gives you access to it in case you need to make repairs. It's the best of both worlds and the best option for the time we have to install it. We *are* here to do a good job. The best job we can. This roof is not a shortcut. It's a smart choice based on the limitations we've got to work with."

She sat back and crossed her arms over her chest. Suddenly, instead of the intelligent woman he'd grown to respect, she was the obstinate *hostile* he'd met in the back of the paint aisle during his first hour in Middleburg. "I'm *trying* here," he said. "What about you? You've been just waiting, just hunting for faults. Sitting back with an 'I told you so' all loaded up the minute you found a target. And somehow, I knew it'd be me."

When this had become so personal, Drew couldn't say. But it was. Highly. "You know, you almost had me," he went on. "I thought maybe we'd finally convinced you that we're not part of the imagined hordes you've decided are out to get you." He paced the bus, trying to get a check on his anger. He had to calm down, pull his tangled emotions out of this, and get her to understand. "We're all making adjustments here. And yes, I'm making compromises, but all compromises aren't bad. As long as we keep our eyes on what can't be compromised, we can understand what can be. Even I'm catching on to that. I'm getting on a plane tomorrow not because I want to, but because it needs to be done. It's a compromise that will get us a huge sponsorship and let us help three times as many people in the next three seasons. And people want our help. People *need* our help. And, hard as it may be for you to admit it, *Middleburg* wants our help." He flung one hand toward the church lawn, his temper getting the best of him again. "Your neighbors are happy to have us here. They see us as an answer to prayer. They pray with us. They pray *for* us. Can't you see that? You won't even come to the prayer meeting and hear people giving up all kinds of thanks to the Lord that He sent us here to help them."

Her eyes turned sharp and cold. "Don't make this about church. Don't you *dare* go there again."

And maybe that's what burned him most of all. You simply couldn't make this about anything but church. This *was* church. The body of Christ, reaching out and helping. He was trying to help in every way he could, and she was standing there, blocking his path in her pursuit of some concept of perfection. *She makes me so angry, Lord. Why won't she see Your hand in this?* He took a deep breath and lowered his voice. "Okay, purely professionally speaking, every single construction project—everywhere on the planet—faces compromises based on time, materials and a gazillion other variables. It's why budgets have contingency lines. You of all people should understand that."

"This is not a lumber shortage or a zoning snafu. Those are compromises. This is cutting corners, pure and simple."

Drew groaned and thumped his hand on the table. "No. This is working with what we've got. This is already far and above what you could have achieved without us. This is such an amazing thing if you'd just take off those idealist blinders and *look around you.*" He leaned over the table toward her, willing her to pull that wall back down, furious that she looked at him with such a cutting suspicion. "Middleburg's little kids are going to have the coolest preschool around. Your church is better off. Why can't you get that? Why do you have to be hunting for how I'm out to con you?" And it had become just that, hadn't it? It had all somehow boiled down to how he was out to trick her. It had become infuriatingly personal.

"Because you're leaving, and I'll be stuck here picking up the pieces." It meant a million things the way she said it.

And it was true. It did mean a million things. The tone of her words cut through his anger to force the realization that he *was* leaving. He'd leave Middleburg when this was over, and he hadn't even realized how it was bothering him. Never before had Drew had so many reasons to rush ahead and so surprising a craving to stay put.

"You can do whatever you want, can't you?" she went on. "Just as long as we think it's wonderful, as long as we don't look too close. Because by the time we see the cracks in the plaster, you'll be gone." She grabbed up her papers, and suddenly they both knew they weren't talking about the cistern or the roof anymore. "You and your shiny happy bus will be long gone into your huge new season and we'll…we'll still be here making the real life happen. The dull, daily stuff you don't have to worry about like how much higher the heating bill will be or how long the carpet stays tacked down. It's easy to leave, Drew. The real work is in staying."

He grabbed her shoulder. "You have *no idea* how hard it is to leave here." His voice tripped over the words even as his grip on her thundered through both of them. Let go, he told himself. Let go of her. He didn't.

She stared at him, her eyes a mixture of puzzlement and awareness, and Drew realized he was slipping down that slope he'd tried so hard to avoid.

She'd gotten to him. Gotten under his skin.

He'd let her resistance egg him on, just as he was always drawn to the hostiles. He let her go.

"What do you mean 'hard to leave'?" She pulled away from him, but her voice lost all its edge. "You've got everything. You're a hero. A star, and soon to be a bigger one at that. I mean, just look at your home." She waved her arms around the bus. "It's got all the bells and whistles. You get every new tool the moment it's made."

"It's a bus," he said blandly. "It's not a home." At that moment, he thought about the little line of trinkets that stood on her kitchen window, the tiny accumulations of a lifetime in one place that she probably never even noticed anymore, and his heart ached. For here, for her, for this ordinary thing he thought could be replaced by all the lights and drama.

You can't have her. This is dangerous. Really, truly dangerous, his spirit yelled silently. "I'm leaving. And it's hard." It explained everything and nothing.

A terrible silence hung in the air. Her eyes burned dark and wounded, and for a single moment he was ready to ditch every conviction and take her in his arms. She'd fit perfectly, too. He just knew it somehow, which made it all the worse.

"Don't make me regret you ever came." She turned and left.

He started after her, then stopped himself. Right under the Home Green Home sign he'd made for the bus back during the first season.

With a growl, he pulled the sign off the nail and tossed it across the bus. It skidded on the carpeting and slid under the back bunk to slam against some boxes. *Lord, You could have ripped* Missionnovation *right out from underneath me and I don't think it would feel this bad.* Drew sank back against the bus wall and fisted his hands in his hair. Why is this falling apart now?

Chapter Seventeen

Drew hardly slept. He bumbled around the bus at three-thirty in the morning, trying to remember if they had an iron somewhere. He didn't have to wear a suit, sure, but he felt like he at least ought to look like he put in an effort to look nice. If he'd been smart, he would have asked Annie where the iron was before she trundled herself off to the bed and breakfast. He didn't want to turn on the light for fear of waking Kevin, but if he hit his toe on one more corner it was going to be a very long day indeed. And he was already fighting to keep a good spirit. Taking a 5:30 a.m. flight to the coast was enough to fry any brain even without his earlier fight with Janet.

Coffeemakers are quiet. Start there. Drew groped his way toward the middle of the bus where the kitchenette and coffeemaker were.

And smiled.

There, hung on a cabinet handle with a Wear This sticky note above it, was a freshly laundered—and neatly pressed—green *Missionnovation* button-down shirt. Next to the coffeemaker, which was already filled with grounds and water so all he had to do was hit the on switch, was a *Missionnovation* travel mug with a second sticky note that simply said "GWG." On the *Missionnovation* bus, that was shorthand for "Go with God." Drew could think of no finer send-off for the very unusual day he had before him. Annie truly was the glue that held *Missionnovation* together. Anyone who thought it was his doing was sorely mistaken. He found the notes he'd left on the counter for Kevin and Annie and wrote "GWG" across the top with a fat black marker.

When the plane landed in Los Angeles, Drew found himself missing Kentucky's gentle, misty sunrises. The sun crept into the day through the Bluegrass mountains, but here, it seemed to explode too loudly off the horizon. Charlie met him at the airport, sporting one of his sharp dark suits and looking every inch the television producer. "How are ya, Charlie?" he said, grabbing Charlie by the arm and feeling like it had been far too long since they'd seen each other. His first season of *Missionnovation*—back before the shirts and buses and coffee mugs—seemed like decades ago. "If our friends could see us now," he joked, adjusting Charlie's tie even though it was perfect already.

"What's in the boxes?" Charlie pointed to the stack of bakery boxes Drew had brought with him on the plane.

"Oh, a few hometown goodies from the site. You haven't lived until you've tasted Muffinnovations."

Charlie looked doubtful that this designer-organic-soy-latte crowd would handle anything called "Muffinnovations."

"They're green," Drew added, just because it made Charlie's eyes bulge a little wider. "Very green. And they're delicious."

"Fine. I'll eat a muffinno-whatever on the way if it'll make you feel better. But I'm going to start praying now. Hard."

"My dad always said a soul prays better on a full stomach."

Janet had a million other things to do today, but she wasn't taking one eye off this roof installation. Especially with Drew out of town. She'd spoken with the roofing men three or four times over the last day, and they had answered several of her concerns to her satisfaction. That made it better, but by no means was she ready to give her approval of the project. So, despite a whopping workload back at the store, Janet cleared her day to stay on site and make sure MCC got the roof it deserved.

The first part of the gutters went up with ease. Things fit where they were supposed to, and Janet grew optimistic. It'd be satisfying to have the thing in and done right by the time Drew returned from California. The second and third sections were trickier, needing to match angles with the first sections, but with a bit of tweaking everything worked. Everything was going according to the timetable Janet and Kevin had drawn up. Janet even caught herself feeling less stressed as she tightened the screws that held a downspout in place.

By two o'clock, Kevin was up on the highest point of the church, working with the roofers in Drew's place to get the flashings around the steeple in an adjustment she'd suggested.

She knew the time because she was checking her watch when she heard it.

Accidents seem to have a sound all their own. Things fall all the time, and the brain recognizes the ordinary nature of the sound. The real crashes, the ones involving loved ones and precious things, register instantly in the brain. Janet knew, the second she heard the sound of splitting lumber, that something bad had happened. She'd caught the eye of the worker next to her—the bank teller here on his day off from work—and froze in alarm. But only for a second, before dropping her screwdriver and bolting around the corner to where the sounds continued in a lengthy, lethal-sounding series of crashes.

Kevin lay motionless on the grass, his body curled in an unnatural angle. His hard hat had rolled off his head, and one arm lay sprawled awkwardly behind him. For a split second Janet thought he was dead, until he made a horrible moaning noise and lurched to one side, followed by a flinch that told her he was in serious pain. The roofers were talking amongst themselves, trying to figure out how Kevin had fallen despite the safety equipment she knew they all used.

Most of the other *Missionnovation* staff were clear across the property working on the pre-school. Janet found herself nearly alone among a handful of people who looked shocked and stumped as to what to do now.

"You," she pointed to the tallest of them, "Call 9-1-1. The address we're at is 128 March Avenue, on the west side of the building." Janet caught sight of her mother coming out of the church's front doors, followed by several other women who must have heard the accident from the inside. "Mom!" Janet shouted, "Go find Annie on the bus and tell her Kevin's been hurt. Tell her to get a hold of Drew in California right away."

Drew stared at the sleek-looking HomeBase marketing executive in front of him, and wondered if the guy would know what to do with a hammer if handed one. Sure, he's slick, but don't judge, Drew thought to himself, God can work with anybody He chooses. After all, he said HomeBase was interested in expanding the show without removing any of the spiritual content.

"We like what we're seeing," the HomeBase rep said. "Good numbers, good exposure. There isn't a whole lot of family-oriented television we can get behind these days. We're glad to be behind *Missionnovation,* and we'd like to take it to the next level."

"If you could just see the kinds of things we've been able to do," Drew said. "Only about half of what we do makes it on the air. Visit a site one of these days, and you'll see just how far your current backing is taking us. Lives are being changed. Whole communities are changing how they feel about the church. About God. It's incredible."

"I'm sure it is." The way he said it, though, Drew was pretty sure the man would never take him up on his offer of a site visit. Charlie was right—these people were too busy to stand in a church basement and watch the new furnace fire up. Everybody's got a different part to play, Drew thought silently. God knows what He's doing and who He's doing it with.

And God was setting gears in motion, no doubt about it. The way Charlie was smiling, they'd have a deal sewn up by sundown, and Drew could get on the red-eye with the happy news that *Missionnovation* was up, running and expanded for three more years.

"We got him," Charlie said after they finished the meeting. "The deal's just signatures away."

Drew shot Charlie a look. "You sound way too much like them sometimes."

Charlie slapped his hands together and closed his eyes. "Dear Lord, we think You've got him. Please, if it be Your will, let the deal be only signatures away."

"Better," Drew commented, "but only by the tiniest bit." He could tease Charlie about praying over things because Charlie had, once he came to faith, become a fierce prayer warrior. Thanks to Charlie's focus, Drew had learned to cover *Missionnovation* in prayer from its earliest days. Drew had learned to balance prayer and action by watching how Charlie did it. Humbling as it was, Drew felt that Charlie was a stronger man of God than he was, even though Drew had been the first to find Christ. They were good for each other—sharpened by the partnership and honed by the friendship. It was what enabled them to have the high level of trust they did.

They were getting ready for lunch when Drew's cell phone rang. It startled him to see Annie's name on the screen—she knew better than to call with anything less than an emergency on a day like today. His throat tightened as he flipped open the phone.

"Annie?"

"Drew, there's been an accident." Annie's voice had the wobbly tone of someone trying to stay calm. The sound of it sent a chill down through his shoes. "Kevin was up on the church roof making Janet's changes to the steeple flashings and he fell off."

Drew shut his eyes and sent a wordless call for help heavenward. *No, Lord! Not while I'm off-site!* If anything happened to Kevin—or anybody, for that matter—Drew didn't know what he'd do.

The fact that Annie hadn't added "But he's okay" to her statement told Drew things were serious. "How is he? How far did he fall?" he gulped into the phone, and the questions made Charlie's eyes shoot up from his paperwork.

"I'm in the ambulance now. He's conscious, but they won't know anything until the X rays."

Annie never cried, but she sounded on the verge of it now. Drew's heart twisted into a knot of regret. Kevin must be seriously hurt for her to be so shook up. How could he ever have convinced himself it was a good idea to leave the site?

"Kevin's tougher than he looks. He'll be okay." The words rang hollow—he barely believed them himself.

"Okay." There was a silence between them. They both knew Kevin might not be okay.

Drew heard Kevin moaning in the background. He heard the strained voice of what must be a paramedic telling Kevin to "Please try and lie still, Mr. Cooper."

"Tell him I broke everything," came Kevin's voice over Annie's phone, the words thick as if his lips were swollen. Drew pictured the worst; Kevin mangled and bruised on an ambulance gurney, bleeding over everything. Annie would be clutching her clipboard and her files of insurance cards and medical histories she always kept in a red folder in the bus office filing cabinet. He should be there.

"Annie." He forced calm into his voice. "It'll be okay. You know Cooper," he tried to joke. "He's always playing things for sympathy." That was a dumb idea—this was no laughing matter. "Charlie will have people praying over Kevin in ten minutes, if not already. I know you can hold it together until I get there."

"I got it covered." Her voice was tense, but level. Even so, it struck him like a rock thrown into his stomach.

"Where's everyone else?" he said, just to keep her talking.

"Mike has the others staying on site. Janet's meeting us at the hospital with some other folks from the church."

Keep her talking, he thought. Keep her listing things that are going the way they should. It's all you can do from here. "Was anyone else hurt?"

"No, just Kevin."

"Ow! Could you stop that?" Kevin howled somewhere in the background. Kevin didn't even like bandages, so he could just imagine what horrors he found inside an ambulance.

"He looks banged up pretty bad." Annie's voice wobbled a bit, but she held on to her composure. "His leg…"

"Let's not speculate, Miss Michaels," came a professionally calm voice. "We're almost there, so you'll need to hang up now. Tell your boss we'll know more in an hour or so."

"I…um…I have to go," Annie said quietly into the phone.

"I hear. Okay, take care of Kevin, and I'm sure

everything will work out. God's looked out for us before, He's not going to stop now. Stay steady."

Drew snapped his phone shut and sank his head into his hands. A tidal wave of worry for his friend, of regret for a possible wrong choice, swept over him with a force that almost made him ill.

"He's seriously hurt. Why did I think it was okay to leave the site?" he said without looking up.

"You didn't cause this." Charlie was choosing his words carefully. "Don't go there."

"Kevin's been a loose cannon for years. He's never careful about safety stuff."

"Which means it was bound to happen sometime, whether you were there or not."

Drew shot him a look. "Don't placate me. Just get people praying and find me a flight out of here."

Charlie gestured toward the open laptop on the table beside him. "I sent out a broadcast e-mail thirty seconds ago. And I've already started looking for flights. I can't get you back to Lexington before nine-thirty this evening. Even if I fly you into Louisville and you drive the rest of the way. Tell Kevin to fall closer to a major metropolitan airport next time."

It was supposed to be a joke to break the tension. It wasn't, and it didn't.

Chapter Eighteen

Doc Walsh came by the hospital emergency room where Janet and Annie were waiting with Kevin after his leg had been cast. Having the local doctor treat Kevin had been her mom's doing. Lexington General Hospital was a fine institution, but Bebe Bishop didn't trust any hospital unless Doc Walsh was there to supervise. "You made of rubber or somethin'?" the white-haired doctor asked as he glanced over Kevin's chart.

Kevin managed something between a smile and a wince. "Could be."

Doc Walsh peered over the top of his thick glasses. "Most people I know would have come out of a fall like that with a lot more than broken bones."

"Well," Kevin offered, "I hurt everywhere."

"You'll have a mighty nice collection of bruises tomorrow, that's for sure." He signed off on some papers that would allow him to go home to the bed and breakfast where Annie was also staying—the narrow confines of the bus were off-limits for two days at least, until Kevin was allowed onto his foot with the aid of crutches. If Janet knew her mother, Bebe already had a full shift of volunteers scheduled to watch over Kevin while he healed. Maybe even keep him in casseroles until he was fifty—the show's catering or the fact that the bed and breakfast could easily feed him wouldn't even be taken into consideration.

"Blue goes nice with green," Annie tried to tease, but her tense voice gave her away. "You always said you thought you looked good in blue."

"*You* said I looked good in blue," Kevin corrected, "and I think bruises are more of a purple than blue. And you already know how I feel about purple."

Janet gave a puzzled look.

Annie smirked. "Nothing. Just an argument we were having yesterday over Alphco's plants."

"Hello there, Bebe." Doc Walsh closed the file and handed the papers back to the nurse. Janet was so busy trying to figure out the series of looks passing between Kevin and Annie that she hadn't even seen her mother walk in. "You got things all set to transport our guest out to the B and B?"

Janet had asked her mom to look around for a bigger car to bring Kevin back from the hospital.

Her Jeep was not exactly conducive to transporting a tall bruised man with a leg in plaster.

"Sandy Burnside's in the parking lot with her Cadillac. You could practically camp out in the backseat of that thing."

"Look," said Annie, taking Janet's elbow, "you've done more than enough already. I'll see to getting Kevin settled in at the B and B. We've hijacked enough of your afternoon. He and I have to go over what we're going to do about the prayer meeting tonight, anyway."

"The prayer meeting!" Bebe exclaimed. "Well of course we'll have it, even if we have to run it ourselves. After all, we've got to pray for Kevin's leg now."

Tell me what to say.

It was an impulsive cry for help.

It was also the first prayer Janet had said in years. Annie, oblivious to the argument Janet had with Drew before he left, had no idea what she was asking when she gave Janet Drew's cell phone number and asked her to call him. Drew answered on the first ring. "Drew, it's Janet."

There was a moment of surprised silence before he said, "How is he? He's okay, isn't he?"

"He'll be okay. They've set the broken leg and done some other things for the broken ribs. All things considered, he's amazingly intact. I mean, for someone who tumbled off a roof." Janet tried to focus on assuring Drew and ignore how awkward this felt given how they'd left things. "He's banged up, but according to Doc Walsh it's mostly bruises except for the leg and ribs. Oh, and I think one finger, too."

"Ring finger, left hand. Annie sends detailed updates on the hour." She heard him sigh. "How is she doing?"

Janet sank down onto a bench outside the hospital entrance. Now that they were talking, she was tired all of a sudden. "Worried, but efficient. Stress kicks her organizational skills into overdrive. She's got things under control."

There was a long pause on the other end of the phone. "I should have been there." His tone was almost as if he was lecturing himself, as if he'd forgotten she was still on the line.

Janet let out the breath she hadn't even realized she'd been holding. "He's going to be okay. He feels like a jerk, if that helps. He's terrified of what you'll do to him when you get back."

"It's not his fault. It's my job to watch out for these people." He groaned. "I hate that I can't get back sooner. There's a jet taking off and landing here every eight seconds, and I can't get myself to Kentucky for another four hours? That's crazy."

He sounded on the verge of his boiling point. Considering what he was supposed to be doing out there, Janet doubted he was anything more than a ticking time bomb at any of those meetings. Charlie had his hands full. She tried humor. "You're just used to living in the center of the universe, that's all."

Another long pause. This is why she tried to talk Annie out of making her call Drew—this wasn't helping at all. She heard Drew mumble on the other end of the line and she imagined him pacing the sidewalk outside a trendy Los Angeles restaurant. The guy could barely sit still under ordinary conditions—he must be like a caged animal right now. *Hey, God, are You listening? I need help here.* "Think of it this way," she started in, not really knowing where she was heading. "God must have something He needs you to do in L.A. over the next four hours. I can't think of any other reason the Lord of the Universe wouldn't be clearing the way for you to get back to us sooner than that. There's just got to be something keeping you there."

No one was more surprised at her comments than Janet herself. She wasn't used to God popping up in her conversations—or prayers or thoughts—anymore. For as long as she'd turned her back on Him, God was under no obligation toward any prayer of hers.

Still, Drew's tone changed completely. "You're right. God is still in control. Kevin already has loads of people praying for him, with more to come after tonight's meeting. It's covered. I need to remember that God's got it covered. You know, Janet, you got a lot of spiritual wisdom for someone who claims she doesn't do church."

If Janet managed to use godly wisdom to keep one highly worried absent friend from losing it, that didn't make her religious again. She was just speaking in his dialect. Still, the notion that God had given her the right words wiggled its way uncomfortably under her skin. She wasn't sure she was ready to find her way back to faith. "Go be smooth and charming and all that Hollywood stuff. Eat tiny organic salads with powerful people in sunglasses or whatever it is y'all do out there in TV land."

Drew gave a soft laugh. "The salads *are* tiny out here. I'd give anything for a steak, mashed potatoes and pie from Deacon's right now. I just had some purple juice smoothie thing to drink with lunch. And just *try* to get a normal cup of coffee out here."

He sounded better already. "When does your flight get in?"

"Ten-fifteen."

"I'll pick you up at the airport." Again, it jumped

out of her mouth unbidden. Where had that come from? Hadn't their last conversation been an argument? Besides, he had people for that sort of thing, he didn't need her for it. "We…um… Deacon's is open late tonight," she backpedaled, "so we can swing by and feed you on your way back to the bus. Kevin's staying at the bed and breakfast where Annie is so people can look after him until he's up and around again." Now she was practically running on at the mouth.

"Man, I'd like that." She heard him fumble with the phone. "Hang on, I've got the flight number here somewhere…flight 2156 touching down at ten-fifteen."

"I'll be there."

"I'll be glad." There was a gaping silence as he realized what he just said. "Um…glad to get out of here," Drew added, but it was a poor cover-up neither of them believed.

Janet said goodbye quickly and snapped her phone shut, sinking onto the bench again.

He felt it. Like it or not, she had unfinished business with Drew Downing. Too much of it.

Janet bumbled through the next few hours, checking in with Annie at the bus and with her mom at the bed and breakfast. Kevin now had an army of church volunteers assembled to nurse him back to health. Annie's composure was unraveling as she realized the prayer meeting now fell solely on her shoulders. When Janet suggested she just cancel the thing given the circumstances, Annie's jaw dropped. "We couldn't!"

"Why not?" Janet retorted. "People can pray anywhere, right? It doesn't need to be a group activity—just tell people to pray for Kevin and the project on their own tonight."

"Not in a million years." Annie said. "Even if Drew wouldn't have my hide—which he would—I'd *want* to gather people to pray when things go wrong. That's the best time to gather people to pray." She sank back against the bus. "I just hate the thought of getting in front of that microphone. I'll get Jeremy to do it."

Janet leaned back against the bus with her. The woman looked petrified, and Janet wanted to help any way she could. "So don't use a mic. Just have people gather like you said. Someone'll start singing if the church choir shows up again anyway. You don't need to make a production of it if that's driving you crazy."

Annie blinked at her. "You're right. There's always more than one way to do a prayer meeting. Why didn't I think of that?"

Janet had to smile. "You would have, just as soon as you caught your breath."

"You should come." It wasn't a manipulative invitation the way Annie said it—it was just a heart-felt statement from one exhausted person to another.

"Not really my thing," Janet said. "Mom'll be there, though. And the whole rest of the church— I mean those that aren't on Kevin nurse duty."

Annie's eyes fell shut and she let her head fall back against the bus wall. "Praise God he's all right. It could have been so much worse. I don't know what I'd do without him."

As Janet finished up with Annie and said good-night, she wondered if Drew realized what was going on between Annie and Kevin. The looks, the fighting. Janet wondered if even they realized how much they cared for each other yet. She caught herself gazing heavenward and asking "What are You up to?" And then she shook herself because it was something she would have done years ago.

Chapter Nineteen

"No offense, but you look awful." Drew had practically shuffled toward Janet, looking drawn and frazzled. Even though it was early for an insomniac like him, he looked like he'd fall asleep the minute he got in the car.

"Longest day of my life. Literally, with the time change and all. I sure hope it was worth it." He slung his jacket over one shoulder and began walking toward the airport exit. "What a blessing not to have to wait for baggage. Get me outta here."

"Did you get what you went for?"

If there was anything between them, he was too tired to show it. Maybe she'd imagined what passed between them when he said how much he was looking forward to seeing her. "I don't know how Charlie does it," he said, shaking his head. "All that negotiating is exhausting. I feel like I ran a marathon and all I did all day was sit around tables talking. How'd the prayer meeting go?" he asked, evidently too wiped out to remember she didn't go to those things.

"Don't know. Didn't hear sirens going off or the bus exploding or angry mobs running through town, so I suppose it went okay. Annie was going to ditch the microphone and lights last time I talked to her, and just have everybody pray. She was too worried about Kevin to do much else."

"I can't believe he got hurt. But he sounds like he'll be okay. I talked to him for a few minutes earlier. He sounds like a guy on large doses of painkillers, but he still sounds like Kevin. He was actually more worried about Annie and the prayer meeting." They had reached the Jeep and he stopped to open the door for Janet. "Those two don't trust each other for nothing."

Janet slid behind the wheel. "You don't see it, do you?"

He climbed into the passenger seat. "See what? My two top teammates scratching each other's eyes out at every opportunity?"

Janet stared at him, narrowing her eyes in disbelief. If even she, who didn't pretend to be any expert at interpersonal relations, caught on to what was going on between Kevin and Annie, how could Mr. Insightful over there miss it by a mile? "Drew," she began, "they're nuts about each other."

Drew chuckled like she'd made a clever joke. "No way."

"How can you not see it? She's completely fallen for him, and I'm pretty sure he's fallen for her. You should have seen them at the hospital. I think even Doc Walsh could see it, and he's pretty clueless in that regard."

Drew's eyes popped wide open. "No! Annie? And Kevin!"

Janet nodded. "You've got an office-bus-whatever romance on your hands the moment they figure it out for themselves. Which, the way they were looking at each other, should be any second now." She checked her watch. "Maybe even already. He is under heavy medication and now they're under the same roof."

"Nah."

She pointed a finger at him as she turned onto the highway toward Middleburg. "I'm telling you. Plain as day."

Drew sat back and ran his hand through his hair. "He did say something odd to me about how she held his hand in the E.R." He fell silent for a moment, and she guessed he was taking a mental inventory of all the times he'd seen the two of them together. "He said something to me about her on the bus the other day. I called her 'my kid sister' and he said 'she's not' in the weirdest way." She caught Drew staring at her out of the corner of her eye as she drove. "I can't believe it, but I think you're right. Good grief, I think you might be right. Never in a million years would I have put those two together."

Why had she brought up the subject of Kevin and Annie's budding romance? Could there be a less appropriate topic of conversation for her and Drew Downing? "Maybe I should just take you back to the bus."

"Oh, no," he moaned, "please get me to some real food. If I don't find some actual meat in the next hour I'll dissolve into a pile of tofu."

She laughed as they were stopped at a red light. "I know just where to take you. There's a great place just outside of Lexington. You haven't lived until you've had a burger from the Parkette Drive-In."

"A drive-in. That sounds like heaven right now. We could pick up something for Kevin, too. He'll be starving when he wakes up off his painkillers and that man does love his cheeseburgers."

She eyed him. "I doubt it will stay warm 'til he gets it."

He grinned. "I doubt he'll care. I'm too desperate to care." He made a face like a dying soldier crawling across a battlefield. "Must…have…real…food." He twitched and fell theatrically against the console between the seats. "Fried things…red meat…soda…"

"We don't call it 'soda' out here, Mister." She reached out to swat him away, but he caught her hand for just a second before releasing it.

"Look, I'm sorry for how we left things. Really," he said, looking like he left much more unsaid. She felt his touch tingle all the way up her arm even when she planted both hands on the steering wheel and glued her eyes to the road. Still, she could feel him looking at her.

Drew polished off the last of his french fries and leaned back, exhausted but supremely satisfied by the down-home meal. The Parkette was just what he needed, one of those good old-fashioned tray-on-the-window drive-through burger joints that were a throwback to the fifties. The last twenty minutes felt like one giant exhale, letting out all the tension of the flight and Kevin's injury and those endless L.A. meetings. "Thank you so much. I needed this."

She chuckled, waving a fry at him. "Need this? No one needs this. I'm not even sure you can call it nutrition—" she popped the fry into her mouth and closed her eyes "—but it sure hits the spot sometimes."

Drew sighed behind a mouthful of burger. "You can't find a burger like this in L.A."

"They do great burgers, but the fish box is their real specialty. Might be more grease, but more pleasure for sure." She watched him close his eyes and sink down in the passenger seat.

"I spent half the flight thanking God for protecting Kevin. It could have been so much worse. Thank God."

That was the thing about Drew. Other people threw phrases like "thank God" into their language so casually. When Drew said "thank God," that's *exactly* what he meant. It wasn't artifice. Drew could see God in everything. There was a time when she was like that.

Tony could take a giant obstacle and make it look like the perfect opportunity for God to show off His mighty power.

It was humiliating to have been so fooled. She'd managed, up until Drew Downing, to keep her skepticism of such leaders firmly in place, her guard firmly up. She didn't know what to do about the fact that she was beginning to believe Drew Downing when he spoke of passionate ideals. She found it very scary territory.

"I spent the other half of the flight realizing

I owed you an apology," Drew went on. "I should have told you about the change to the roof differently."

"I don't think you should have changed it at all," she replied, and she watched him pull in a breath to start in on a defense. "But can we not get into that right now? Let's just leave it at 'apology accepted' for tonight."

"Vern told me you used to go to the church. He told me I had to ask you why you didn't anymore. What happened, Janet?"

She took a deep breath. It probably was time to let Drew know her history—but she'd leave out her personal relationship with Tony. It was enough that Drew would know why she no longer felt an allegiance to the church. "Tony Donalds happened. Actually, Tony's ministry happened—or never happened, but I'm getting ahead of myself."

She stole a look at Drew, to gauge his response, but he simply settled in against the seat to listen. "He was a dynamic guy, and the son of our pastor at the time. Girls joined the youth group just to be around him. Captain of the football team, big college career. People loved him. One of those natural-born leaders you just know is going to go places. So after college, it seemed natural that he'd launch into mission leadership somewhere. Off he went to raise mission support for this dynamic youth program he was going to open out East. Everyone at our church knew he'd succeed. We were praying for him, getting ready for him to come home long enough for us send him off on a great ministry." She stopped, taking a breath under the excuse of a sip of her milkshake. Middleburg was getting ready to send them off—she and Tony as a couple—but she wasn't going to go into that. Drew didn't need to know that her fall from faith included a first-class heartbreak.

"Go on," Drew said quietly.

"He said he didn't want to raise support from around here because he knew God would send him other donors, and we believed him. Tony was that kind of guy. You believed whatever he said." She slipped her shake back into the Jeep's cupholder. "I suppose it should have been the first red flag, but no one was looking for red flags. We were too busy being amazed and impressed." She looked up, and Drew had gone completely still, his gaze locked on her. "Tony's ministry was all bright lights and big plans," she continued, "but that was all he was." She looked down for a moment, unable to say this part with Drew's eyes on her. "Tony wouldn't raise money in Middleburg because some part of him couldn't stomach stealing from his own. So he stole from other people. Took every cent he'd raised for his ministry and disappeared. We didn't make it public—what was the point in destroying everyone's faith? Why spread the pain around? It was bad enough for those of us who knew. Nothing shoots a hole in someone's faith like a big fat case of criminal fraud to your own church by your own pastor's son."

"Wow. I had no idea. I'm sorry."

That's what the few people who knew always said. They'd kept it quiet for just that reason—no one could change what happened anyway. To her or to Middleburg Community Church.

Drew stared at Janet. What she'd told him explained so much. And she'd finally told him, which meant she was turning back toward God in tiny degrees she probably didn't even recognize herself. That ignited his enthusiasm to nudge her further—but knowing her disillusionment, he was going to have to be incredibly careful about that. As much as he wanted to prove to Janet that one man's faults didn't condemn an entire faith, he knew it'd be best if he left her alone. Trouble was, Drew wasn't sure he could. She pulled a determination out of him that was different than other hostiles. He felt a sort of burden for her that went beyond the theological. Beyond the professional. His high-stress time in L.A. had only heightened his awareness of it. When he'd walked off the plane and seen her there, his whole being registered the most surprising sense of relief that she'd still talk to him.

At first he put it down to needing to get back to the work site, needing to make sure Kevin was okay. But as they sat in her car, Drew realized a huge part of his tension was the need to put things right between them. Between her and the church. To heal her. To just plain be *near* her. And that was dangerous indeed. He needed to be very, very careful about the two of them. And late at night, in a dark car with a pretty girl, was a mighty difficult place to be careful.

I'm a mess, Lord. Do something.

As if she'd heard his silent prayer, Janet said, "It's late," and started the engine to head toward town.

Chapter Twenty

Drew was still shaking his head over the awkwardness of his good-night to Janet when the church volunteer on "Kevin duty" led him into the parlor of the bed and breakfast. It was a scene that left him shaking his head even more.

Kevin was set up in a sleeper sofa in the first floor parlor, a bag of quickly gathered clothing and such tossed into a nearby corner. A folding tray by the bed held a glass of water, some bandages, a tube of ointment and a prescription bottle. One of Annie's trademark sticky notes clung to the bottle, with "2:00 p.m., 6:00 p.m., 10:00 p.m." written on it. Even if he didn't recognize Annie's precise handwriting, it wouldn't have been hard to figure out who'd been tending to Kevin; the volunteer silently smiled and pointed to Annie asleep on a chair in the corner. She was out as cold as Kevin.

Neither of them stirred as the volunteer gathered up her knitting and went to sit in the next room. Tonight, they'd all stay at the B and B—not only did Drew want to be close to Kevin, but he felt like he needed an hour-long shower in a real bathroom, not that plastic two-by-two closet that passed for a shower on the bus.

"Hey," Kevin's whisper spun Drew around. "You made it in okay." He sounded rather chipper for someone in his condition.

Drew smirked. "More than I can say for you. Does it hurt?"

"Not much right now." Kevin nodded toward the table of medicine. "But I've got a lot of chemistry going on. Tomorrow'll be another story." He held up the splinted finger. "I'm already turning cool colors."

Annie shifted in her sleep, and Kevin made a tender sound. "I told her to go sleep upstairs. It's not like I'm mortally wounded here." He got a slightly smitten look on his face, the sort of sleepy-eyed smirk produced by a good memory. "She was amazing."

It hit him as if he'd just put on a pair of glasses— Janet was right. Those two were nuts about each other. How on earth could he have missed it? It was like a neon sign between them now that he knew. Had they figured it out themselves? Or was this one of those proverbial love-hate matches where Kevin and Annie would be the last to know? "Why don't I go upstairs, grab a quick shower, then I'll come back down and take the night shift so Annie can get some decent sleep."

"She was amazing," Kevin repeated, a little fuzzier this time. "Hey, what's in the bag?"

Drew had forgotten the bag still in his hands. "Medicinal cheeseburgers. Can't have my buddy taking painkillers on an empty stomach."

"Gimme that." Kevin reached for the bag until a wince stopped him. "You ever broken a rib before? It really hurts."

Drew brought the bag closer and moved the tray table so that it was easily within Kevin's hampered reach. "I can only imagine. I think you're benched for the duration. You want us to fly you back home?"

"No unnecessary air travel for forty-eight hours," came Annie's yawning voice behind Drew. "We've got to put up with his moaning until he goes home with the rest of us."

"I'll have you know I'm seriously injured." Kevin called out as he dug into the bag for his burger.

Annie sat up and put her glasses back on. "Yes, you are. So take it seriously and stop moving around so much."

Oh, those two had it bad for each other, all

right. If only Drew stood a chance of surviving the crossfire.

"I'm going to go take a shower and then I'll take the night shift, Annie."

"I think I know how much I can…" Kevin reached for something on the table and then hissed in pain. "Okay, maybe I ought to take it a bit slower. You don't give your ribs a second thought until you bust one."

"See, you can't just go twisting around like that in your condition. You're supposed to be lying still, remember? And when's the last time you drank some water?"

She was still at it when Drew hit the top of the stairs. *Oh, Lord, I want them happy, but I liked it a lot better when they hated each other.*

Drew sat in the bus the next morning, flow-charts spread around the table in front of him. Things were always tight the last week on the job, but now with Kevin on the disabled list, things were beyond tight. Not to mention that as land-scaping guru, the last week was usually where Kevin had the most input. Now, the most he could manage was to have Kevin supervise a team of volunteers from a patio chaise longue with his foot propped up. Not exactly the optimum scenario. *Time to be the Big God,* Drew prayed as he sank his head into his hands. *We got a heap of problems and not a heap of solutions to throw at them.* As Drew stared at the demanding time-tables, a string of all-nighters seemed to stare back at him. This would be full tilt 24-7 to pull off.

Those kinds of time frames didn't faze him, however. Pulling it off at the last minute was part-and-parcel of *Missionnovation's* excitement. The pressure always pulled new and better things out of Drew. The last-minute all-night papers were always his best in college, he often started his Christmas shopping on December 23. Drama aside, it was Drew's calm under fire that enabled *Missionnovation* to keep its nail-biter schedule. As far as Drew was concerned, there was always enough time to find a solution, even if you only had two hours. There had been episodes in some seasons where the clean-up crew had been pulling trash bags out the back door at the same moment Drew had been handing over the keys at the front door. The first time it happened, Annie stayed behind in the bus, breathing into a paper bag. By the third season, Annie was calmly distributing trash bags with one hand while handing Drew the keychain with the other. Everyone had somehow grown used to chaos as standard operating procedure. *We've done it before, Lord. Remind me we can do it again. Send me some encouragement to fuel my weary soul.*

As if by divine command, Drew's cell phone buzzed in his pocket. It was still on vibrate from his all-night vigil over Kevin. Kevin's prediction that his injuries would be worse in the morning was dead on; the man woke up as a human crash site, grumpy and claiming even his teeth were hurting him. Looking at the collection of bumps, bruises and stitches that was his teammate, Drew was drawn once again to a gush of thankfulness that Kevin hadn't been more seriously hurt.

"God caught him when he fell," Annie said when Drew told her at breakfast how thankful he was that Kevin hadn't been more seriously injured. Now that he realized it, Drew felt like those two were wearing their hearts on their sleeves—it was surely only a matter of days if not hours before they figured it out for themselves, in which case the bus was going to feel like a rolling valentine.

Not exactly the best place for a particular guy trying to forget what he was feeling for a particular lady.

Drew flipped open the phone to see Charlie Buchanan's office line on the screen. A little good news from the west coast might be just the ticket to an energizing day. "What's up, Charlie."

"I've got great news, but first, how's Kevin?"

"Much better when the pain medicine kicks in.

He's banged up, but it could have been tons worse given how far he fell. So let's hear the good news."

"We got 'em. HomeBase is formalizing a sponsorship offer for the next three seasons of *Missionnovation.* An outstanding offer. If we can get you out here soon, they're ready to ink a very sweet deal. Are you ready to become a household name, Drew? Because if they take it as far as they're talking, you will be. You know that line of eco-friendly products you've been thinking of? I happened to mention it to them after you left the other time, and they're showing lots of interest. They're talking about a whole promo on native wildflowers like Kevin always insists on using. And they're one hundred percent behind keeping the emphasis on faith. The whole *Missionnovation* vision—they've caught it."

Drew sank back in his chair. Full funding, somebody behind his vision—including the God part—and no budget worries for three years. That was serious expansion. "That's…incredible. Amazing. I knew you could do it, Charlie." Drew hoisted the mug he was holding. "Well, hello and God bless 'ya, HomeBase."

"Use that line a lot when you get out here. They want to announce it at their annual shareholders' meeting on the twentieth. If we get all the *i*'s dotted and *t*'s crossed by then."

Something at the very edge of Charlie's tone caught in Drew's ear. "Meaning?"

"Well, we've got a bit of fine print to iron out on this one. When the deals get this big, the details get complicated."

And that, without a doubt, was "Charlie-speak" for *You may not like what I say next.*

"Meaning?"

"They've actually offered above and beyond what we proposed, Drew. We'll go from a well-done minor show to a very big league major network sensation. And they're not asking us to water down the faith, Drew. Not a bit. Do you understand how big that is? What kind of visibility they're handing us? Even in all my planning, I never thought we'd get this far." Charlie paused before he continued. "They're demanding an exclusive, Drew. But we won't need anyone else's backing with this offer. This is it. This is our shot. It's a whole new world from here on in."

"Wow." How was it supposed to feel, to *arrive?* To achieve something he'd worked so long to obtain? Drew stood up and paced the bus, unsure how to feel. Exhilarated? Scared? Blessed beyond his imagination? At the moment, Drew felt like he'd just been shot out of a cannon. But God's eye was on the sparrow, right? And that could always be trusted.

"Exclusive, huh?"

"Exclusive. Only one phone call to get whatever you need, whenever you need it."

"Wow," he said, unable to come up with a more creative response. "That's huge."

"It is, Drew. Enormous. Think of it—God just did something so enormous even *I'm* not able to take credit for it."

"Just when I thought I couldn't find a way to describe how big it is," Drew teased. He imagined Charlie'd been dancing in his office, celebrating. "Maybe I should crack open four boxes of Dave's for breakfast instead of my usual two."

"Yeah," said Charlie, a bit nervously. "You might want to eat up your supply this season."

Drew practically pulled the phone away from his ear to stare at it in disbelief. "No Dave's?"

"That's what exclusive means, Drew. It means nobody else's products appear but HomeBase's."

"But HomeBase doesn't make cookies, Charlie. I'm fine with using all their tools and appliances and stuff, but I don't know how to run a show without Dave's cookies."

Drew heard Charlie sigh on the other end of the phone. "Nobody says you have to stop eating Dave's. You'll just have to buy your cookies and eat them off-camera from now on—and believe me, you'll have a big enough budget to keep yourself in cookies."

"But at the end of the show…the milk and cookies…"

"Look, there's a lot of creative minds in on this. I'm sure we can find an alternative that'll make everyone happy." He paused again, and Drew heard some papers shuffling in the background. "Keep the big picture in mind here. This is worth it. A full eighteen episodes *and* a Christmas special, not to mention print advertising in more magazines than you and I could read in a lifetime. For a *Christian* show."

Annie had always wanted to write a home-organizing column. Maybe now they'd have the leverage to make that happen. And Kevin would get all the native species plants he wanted. The whole team would never have to make do again—and they all had jobs for the next three years. With that kind of job security, maybe even Kevin and Annie could end up at the altar.

"Drew?" Charlie's voice pulled him back. "About that shareholders' meeting?"

"Yeah, I heard you say something about that." Drew ran his hands through his hair, thinking he might need to shake his head to clear the tangle of thoughts going through it right now.

"It's on the twentieth. I need you to commit to

it today. Now, if you can. You'll have the season wrapped by then, won't you?"

Drew glanced at the pile of production schedules he'd been scouring when Charlie called. "Um…it's a bit tight with Kevin out of commission, but…" he flipped through two more pages, checking half a dozen deadlines "…yeah, we can do it. Tell 'em we're on. You've got legal on all the paperwork?"

"You'll get a package by this afternoon to look over, another one for your signatures on Monday. Did I mention you've still got full control of the cast and crew?"

"No, but I'm glad to hear it. What about the bus? Am I going to live in a HomeBase delivery truck now or something?"

"Bus*es,* my good man. *Plural.* Three. One for you, two for the expanded team."

Drew leaned back against the filing cabinets. "And what do *you* get, Chuck?"

"I get the best part of all, Drew. I get to be the guy who made it happen. Aside from God, of course, but lots of folks in this neighborhood haven't figured that out yet. *Yet.* God's credentials just went up threefold in TV land."

Be careful what you pray for. The platitude rang in Drew's head as he tried to take in what his future now held. *Missionnovation* would be bigger and better than ever before.

Would it?

Bigger, yes. But Drew wished he could be more certain about how much better it would be. A part of him wondered if he could keep the personal touch—the one-on-one connection that fueled him—on the grand scale *Missionnovation* would now have. He thought about matching up the artisans for the preschool garden. The stone-mason whose family had been in the business for three generations and the blacksmith who made a gate especially for those little kids. The painter. And Janet.

What he'd told Janet was right; *Missionnova-tion* needed both the big chain stores and the small local shops. Could it be the same show with just HomeBase? Granted, HomeBase was filled with people, too, maybe even with unique craftsmen and folks who cared about building things like no one had ever seen—was he right to stereotype them as an uncaring conglomerate just because they were big? Could he lead the team that would strike that all-important balance?

God was leading him into new territory, no doubt about it. Drew just wished he could be more certain it wasn't a detour.

"*How* big?" Kevin's eyes flew wide open when Drew shared Charlie's packet of papers with the team and told them the budget they'd have for next season. "Are all those zeros for real?"

"Three buses?" Annie ran her fingers down a column of figures.

"Exclusive sponsorship evidently has its privileges." Drew fingered a bag of Dave's chocolate chip cookies. "And a few downsides."

"No Dave's?" Kevin reached over and clutched the bag protectively.

"Well, no free Dave's. But a bigger food budget so we can buy all the Dave's we want."

"But…" Annie heard the hesitation in his voice and looked at him from over the top of her glasses.

"But that also means no milk and Dave's at the end of the show."

"Aw, come on," Mike groaned, putting down the wiring he had been fiddling with all through the meeting. Ever since gaining Vern's approval, Mike had become much more confident. And opinionated. "It's not like HomeBase sells milk and cookies and Dave's is their archrival."

Everyone stared. Outbursts from Mike took a little getting used to. "Cookies or no," Drew said, "God's still in control here, and I'm trying to keep open to whatever He's got in mind for *Missionnovation*."

Mike's expression remained sour.

"Think of it this way," Drew suggested, "We're

getting the funds to improve Dave's bottom line by buying the cookies now."

"Yeah," Mike muttered, "that'll more than make up for the lack of national television exposure." The new Mike had more than enough opinions and suddenly wasn't reluctant to share them. Who knew a place like Middleburg would bring this out in the guy? Drew had to wonder what other surprises the next *Missionnovation* season had in store.

"Our main focus right now needs to be completion of the preschool and getting this season wrapped up." After ticking through all the remaining elements of the construction, Drew turned to Kevin. "I'm going over the rest of the roof installation. Can you have another go at the cistern specs? Janet Bishop's not happy with either of them yet."

"Let her talk to Howard Epson," Annie offered. "He's so gung-ho on the cistern thing he's been touting it to every environmental group in the state. He called it 'a civic showpiece' the other day." She rolled her eyes. "He wants a photograph of himself holding the giant watering can as if he were pouring it."

Kevin chuckled and nudged her. "Why did I just know Howard would want to get his hands on 'God's watering can'?"

Drew watched Annie nudge him back. How had

he not seen this before? "Just promise me you'll give them another once-over. Make sure everything's in shape."

"Sure. But it's gonna be tight just getting everything done by the nineteenth as it is. You sure you want to mess with anything now?"

Of course he didn't want to mess with anything now. The HomeBase shareholders meeting was hanging over his head as it was. But he just couldn't get Janet's disapproval out of his head— and she was right, roofs were important.

"Just make sure. We haven't won her confidence, and I'm leaving no stone unturned."

"You know," Mike piped in again, "she'll be the last."

"The last what?" Annie asked.

"The last local vendor. It'll all be HomeBase from here on in. She knows her stuff. You gotta wonder if we'll get folks like that from HomeBase." He sounded an awful lot like Vern.

Drew ignored Mike's last remark. "Get back to me by four o'clock with ways to shave ten hours off our timelines. It's 24-7 now until we hand over the keys, got it?"

Chapter Twenty-One

Janet pulled the final birdhouse off the shelf and blew a layer of dust off the little red roof. It was two days before they'd need the birdhouses, but she'd been unable to sleep since dinner with her mom, and she thought she'd get up and pack the houses rather than lay staring at the ceiling for another hour.

Bebe had gone on and on about the spectacular new preschool. You'd have thought God himself had put up those walls, the way she raved about them. As a matter of fact, to hear her mom put it, God himself did put up those walls. *Missionnovation* was no less than the hand of God to Bebe Bishop. God's chosen messengers of renovation.

Everyone was on cloud nine about the show and the preschool.

Why not her?

Do you have to be such an ungrateful spoilsport? she asked herself as she used a dry paintbrush to get the dust off the tiny white window shutters. Drew is right—this is twice the school we'd be able to build ourselves. Since when did you start caring so much about that church again, anyway?

Her mom had said much the same thing when she dared to raise the topic of the less-than-perfect cistern at dinner. "God's hand is on this, honey. I think He can tend to His own watering can." After that, Janet didn't dare bring up the subject of the roof.

Bebe offered, as she did with most problems, to "pray over it." Somehow Janet failed to see how prayer was a substitute for good project management, but she'd lost that argument with her mother years ago.

It was near three o'clock in the morning, but she could still see the floodlights on over at the church from her kitchen window. They'd talked about working round the clock on their shows before. They were sure burning the candle at both ends this week. Ambitious didn't even begin to cover it. It was bordering on insane.

Without really thinking about it, Janet pulled on a sweatshirt and a pair of jeans. Why not head over there? It couldn't be any worse than insomniac birdhouse dusting.

She wandered through the site, saying hello to this volunteer and that person. She didn't know what fool handed Howard Epson a staple-gun at three in the morning, but he seemed to be holding his own as he tacked carpeting down to a set of risers. Two of her favorite customers—a young couple who'd bought a fixer-upper on the east end of town—were grouting tile on the sink back-splash. The man who ran a tack shop just up the street was painting a pair of pint-sized tables. She noticed a cup of coffee and a half-eaten Muffin-novation on the sawhorse behind him and laughed to herself. So many people out in the middle of the night just to lend a hand.

Unsurprisingly, she ended her wandering at the preschool windows, staring at the little circular garden outside.

Drew was there.

He didn't see her. He was angled away from her with his head down, pressing both hands against the giant watering can as if he were holding it in place. Somehow, without even knowing how she knew, she was certain he was praying over it. The way his shoulders seemed to lean into the casing, the way his fingers flexed against the wall in something that could only be described as a struggle. It was like he was wrestling with the cistern. Or himself.

It was a side of him she'd never seen. And it unnerved her that she could see it so clearly—she didn't think she knew him well enough to see so much strain in his body language. Drew Downing, unstoppable force of nature, was struggling. She saw him lay his head against the wall of the cistern and something enormous twisted in her heart.

He turned, startled, and she realized she'd put her hand up against the glass without even knowing it. His eyes. Maybe that was how he won people so easily—those eyes were so powerful you couldn't hope to pull yourself out of their gaze.

He stared at her for a long moment, over the distance of the garden and the window bay, and the enormous thing in her heart twisted further until she found it hard to breathe. Then, with a deep breath, he shook his head in a laughing, sort of surrendering expression and motioned for her to come outside.

He had good reason to be surprised—she was amazed herself to be standing in a preschool garden in the middle of the night. "I couldn't sleep." It was dumb, and a bit obvious, but it was the only thing that came to mind after the shock of seeing him in so private a moment.

He leaned back against the watering can and tucked his hands in his jeans pockets. He shook his head again. "I was just asking God what to do about you."

How do you respond to a statement like that? It rattled her in a dozen ways. "What'd He say?"

"He didn't say much, but then again I didn't realize you were going to show up in a matter of seconds, so maybe He didn't need to say much."

So he wasn't praying over the cistern, he was praying over her. Just when she thought she couldn't get more unnerved. Janet sat down on the concrete bench shaped like a tree stump. She couldn't pretend anymore that *it*—whatever *it* was between them—didn't exist. She tried to pull the conversation back to something more controllable. "You talk to God about your hardware vendors?"

His expression showed that he knew what she was trying and wouldn't go for it. "I talk to God about everything." He paused a moment before he added, "Including women."

Janet wasn't ready to go in this unsafe direction. "I hate to break it to you," she said as matter-of-factly as she could, "but the Lord Almighty did not raise me out of bed and command me to go see Drew Downing."

He took on a mischievous look, and she saw the grin that won thousands of hearts each week. "You sure?"

"We don't exactly speak much."

The high voltage grin vanished and his voice softened to something more personal. "Want to talk about that some more?"

"No."

"I do. I want to know why you don't talk much to God anymore. I want you to tell me what it was that happened to you."

"Why? So you can fix it? I already told you."

"You told me why you don't go to *church* anymore. I don't think that's the whole story. I think it's more personal than some guy committing fraud."

Drew slid down the side of the cistern until he was sitting on the ground. "I want to understand it. It's not hard to figure out someone hurt you, Janet. You've got a wall four feet thick where men of faith are concerned, and those kinds of things don't spring up out of nowhere."

"You want the whole story? Fine, I'll tell you." Maybe now really was the time to let him know how deep that wound went. It might finally stop his pressure. Janet settled herself on the bench. This didn't condense down to a short story. "You're right, I've got a sore spot for people like you. I earned my thick wall. Or rather, had it given to me."

Drew stretched his legs out and crossed one ankle over the other, settling in as well. She was thankful he didn't try to close the distance between them. "Tony Donalds?"

"We were…involved." She fumbled with the words. It had been years since she'd talked about this with anyone but Dinah and Emily.

"Serious?" Drew cocked his head to one side.

"Ring shopping, if that's what you mean by serious. We were planning to announce our engagement after he'd raised all his mission support. I was really, really involved in MCC at the time, if you haven't guessed. But when Tony did…what he did, it all came undone. Everything I knew about him, everything I knew about faith and serving and integrity…was gone. I had no idea if any of it was true. I loved him. I wanted so much to be part of the amazing future ahead of him." Janet hated how the words caught in her throat, how it made her feel weak and wounded to talk about Tony. "Tony never came back for me because he never came back at all." She felt the old hurt surge back as if the news had come yesterday. "So you'll forgive me if I've learned not to trust a charming man with big ideas who claims God is on his side. I've seen too much to take anyone high and mighty at their word."

She expected him to make some high-intensity response, to jump in and tell her that jerks like Tony didn't represent how real men of God conducted themselves. She'd heard enough of such responses from the few people who really knew why she and Tony broke it off. The fraud was one thing, but to have the brutal heartbreak on top of it—well, she'd never worked up the ability to forgive God for all that pain. The mighty, loving God she'd once known no longer fit into a scheme that included such pointless injustice.

Drew, however, said absolutely nothing. As a matter of fact, it was the first time she'd seen him still and silent since he came into town. Good, she thought. Now you know. All of it. Now you'll back off.

"So," she said, when he still didn't reply. "Now you know."

"I'll spare you the few choice adjectives running through my head at the moment," he said in a dark tone she'd not heard from him before. "It might not improve your already fine opinion of me."

"You're better than most," she offered half-heartedly.

"So are most of us. It burns me to hear about guys like him. So many people are trying to do the right thing and some guy like that comes along and undoes a million good deeds. Shreds people's faith in ways that take years to repair."

Or not repair at all, Janet added silently. She thought about leaving, about getting up and just walking away from Drew now that he knew, but something in the way his back pushed against the cistern behind him made her stay. She knew he was burning up behind those eyes, reaching for some persuasive theological comeback, but in the end he just looked down and kicked some muck off his boot. "All the more reason to do the right thing here, isn't it? The last thing you need is one more guy in here messing things up." After a moment, he looked up at her. "Don't lump me in with that jerk. I've made my share of goofs, and I have no idea how to convince you that if I tell you I care about you, then I really mean it. But that's the whole point, isn't it? Janet, I'm at a loss for how to handle this."

She ought to pretend she didn't know what he meant by that. That she didn't hear the phrase "care about you." "What do you mean 'this'?"

"It's been a crazy week and I'm so tired I could lie down and sleep a week this second…" He paused. "But there's something I want here even more that I *can't have*." He pulled his hands from his pockets and braced them against the tank wall behind him. "I think you already know why things have been so tough between us. Why we fight. You and I…we can't…and I'm not exactly handling it well. That's my fault, and I'm sorry."

Janet couldn't bring herself to reply. She gripped the bench and tried to deny what he was suggesting—what he'd already said—but found she couldn't. What point was there in denying it anyway? They'd known how they felt about each other back on the bus the night before he left. Talking about it only made it worse. Only complicated things. Didn't he know that?

"You're right. There's a huge part of me that wants to jump in here and make everything better. But you and I know that won't happen. It can't happen, actually. Even if I weren't leaving…and I am leaving…I have no business getting into a relationship with someone who doesn't share my faith." After a long moment, he added, "But you did once, I think you still can and I can't believe how much I'd like to ditch my convictions right now and show you what it could really be like. But that's egotistical and unwise, and I'm not handling things well now as it is. I'm sorry I've added to your list of lousy men of faith."

She panicked, blindsided by his confession. "There's nothing happening between us."

"Don't," he said, almost wincing. "Don't tell me something's not there because I think that would just make it worse. I need to do the right thing here—especially knowing what I know now." He looked straight into her eyes. "But you feel it, don't you?"

The thing twisting in Janet's chest threatened to overtake her. "It doesn't really matter, does it?"

"Maybe I should never have said anything—" he raked his hands through his hair "—but when you showed up just as I was praying…I'm tired, I'm not thinking straight, and I'm really attracted to you. I just thought we might fight less about the other stuff if we put our cards on the table about this."

"Wait a minute." Janet stood up off the bench. "You think my reservations about the roof and the cistern are about something between us? That's really low of you." The thought infuriated her— every bit of discrimination she'd ever endured as a female hardware store owner roaring back to life.

"No!" He rose to his feet. "I thought maybe if you knew how much I thought of you, how much I think I feel for you, how hard it is for me…"

"That what? It would make it easier for both of us? Does this feel any easier? How did you think I would take a comment like that?" She couldn't believe she was choking up.

"I don't know." He began pacing. "I don't know what to do about you."

"How about nothing?" she fired back, pacing also. "There's nothing to do. You'll make your shiny, happy miracles and go on. I'll go on with my ordinary life."

He stopped pacing and looked at her. "It's not ordinary. *You're* not ordinary."

She turned to him. "Do you really think I believe that? Don't you think I've seen more than enough of the dazzle you people claim to have?" She put one hand to her chest. "Look at me, look around you. This isn't where someone like you sticks around. I'm not blond and sleek and full of empowering faith. I'm just trying to get by. Just hanging on. Because that's what ordinary life is like, Drew. Just getting by."

Drew jabbed a finger at her. "Will you stop lumping me in with some stereotype you've managed to create for my world? For my faith? I care about you. I thought you should know. Maybe it was a dumb idea, but I thought it would let you see that I think of this place—of you—as anything but ordinary." He let his hand drop. "Why can't you see that?"

"Because no matter what you say to me, you're still leaving." Her voice caught on that last word, and she hated the weakness she was showing. "You're leaving," she repeated, "so it doesn't matter what you say because you don't have to stick around and live up to it. So don't placate me by trying to, okay? Just make your miracles and leave me alone. Don't come back. Even if that stupid tank breaks and the roof starts leaking next week, don't ever come back."

* * *

Janet turned and left the garden, pushing through the school doors and rushing blindly back through the church. She battled unwanted tears, angry that she could be hurt by the denial of something she'd never wanted to want in the first place. She had a thick skin most of the time, but he'd managed to get under it. He told her he cared about her, and she wanted to believe him. After all Tony had done to her, it infuriated her that she could even think of Drew—or his mission—in that way. She didn't want to open up that part of her heart or let faith seep its way back into her soul ever again. The chance for pain was far too great, and she'd barely survived the last wounds.

And so she ran from him, from the church he was rebuilding, from what his eyes made her want again. She rushed through the building and lawn until she found herself gasping at the edge of the parking lot. Janet stared down the darkened street toward Ballad Road. She couldn't go home, he might try to find her there, and she didn't want to talk to him again. Right now the urge to climb in her Jeep and leave the county for the next week until this whole thing went away was so powerful, the only thing stopping her was that she didn't have her car keys. Stumped, she checked her watch. Three-thirty.

Dinah would be up. She started baking at four. She would not cry. Not over him. Not over this. Taking a deep breath, Janet wiped her eyes with the back of her hand and set off toward the bakery.

"What's wrong?" Dinah came to the door in yellow striped pajamas. Her alarmed expression looked lost on a face framed with frizzy red pigtails. "What on earth could put you here at this hour?"

"Not what, *who*. Please tell me you've got some coffee on."

"And you want coffee, too? Get on back to the kitchen, girl. I can't leave the bread but you've obviously got a long story to tell me." She noticed Janet's assessment of her clothing. "I wasn't expecting company."

"I wasn't expecting to be blindsided at three in the morning, so that makes two of us."

Dinah stopped in her tracks. "You were in a car accident?"

"No, it's not like that." Janet walked behind Dinah through the public part of the bakery, back through a beaded curtain to the warm, cinnamon-scented kitchen. She plunked herself down on one of the stainless steel stools and planted her elbows on the table.

"Drew Downing. Well, actually more than Drew Downing, but mostly him."

"Gotten to you, has he?" Dinah stared at her as she moved a tray of dough in loaf pans. She picked up a brush and started coating the top of the dough with what looked like melted butter.

Janet rolled her eyes. "No. Well, maybe. But nothing's going to come of it. It's all so complicated. It's more than just him, it's the whole faith-church-*Missionnovation* thing. It's the roof and the cistern…"

"And God."

Janet spoke right over that remark "…and the way he acts, and what they're doing over there…"

"And God."

"And Tony and all that happened back then…"

"And God."

"Will you *stop* that? You're as bad as he is, making this about something it isn't."

Dinah stopped brushing and put one hand on her hip. "You're smarter than that, Janet. Wake up and realize you're getting all riled up about him and the roof and whatever else because it's stirring up all that stuff you like to pretend is gone. Only God doesn't work like that. You can't stuff Him into one man's mistakes and expect Him to stay there. He goes after His lost ones. Always has."

She'd gone to the wrong friend. Emily was always so much nicer about all this faith stuff.

Dinah could be as relentless as Drew, even if she had held it in where Janet was concerned. Evidently, she was tired of holding it in. "Come on, not you, too. I don't need to hear this now."

Dinah put down the brush. "No, I think now is *exactly* the time for you to hear this. Look, I know that man is fine looking, but you go deeper than that. I watched you watch him the other day—when you didn't know I was looking. It's not the man you find irresistible. It's the faith inside the man."

Janet got up and paced the room, deeply uncomfortable. "I can't have that kind of faith anymore. Tony saw to that."

"You'd put God in that small a box? Unable to restore the gift of faith He gave you—gave you even before you fell for Tony?"

"You think I want it this way? You think I'm enjoying all this pain?"

Dinah squared off at her. "Actually, yes." Janet glared up at her, unable to keep a lid on her agitation. "Well, I do. I think you've gotten so used to your pain that it's safer to stay there. Only now Drew and all his team have stirred everything up. With all this building stuff and his enthusiasm, it got so you couldn't help but be involved. And that made you crazy, because suddenly you've started wanting the church you were so sure you didn't need anymore."

Janet didn't have a response for that. It seemed

all wrong and all too right at the same time, and she was already so confused.

Dinah walked toward her. "I'm not telling you anything you don't already know. Down deep somewhere. Why is it so hard to think God would pull out all the stops to bring you home to church again?"

"Then why didn't He send someone who'd do the job right?" Janet raised her voice despite the early hour. "Why are we fighting about shortcuts and compromises and all the things I can't stand? Drew is too much like Tony."

"You know, I don't think that's it at all," Dinah said. "I think Drew isn't anything like Tony. He's what Tony should have been. He's what it could be like—life and faith and love. And that scares you to death, sugar, whether you're ready to admit it or not."

Chapter Twenty-Two

Measure twice, cut once. One of the basic laws of construction. Drew had measured three times, and he still cut the piece of wood to the wrong length. He'd been beyond useless since Janet Bishop had left him in the garden. *What is going on, Lord? I was sure when she showed up that we were supposed to talk it out. And that guy? How'd You let that happen? Look at all the damage he's done. That talk was supposed to clear things up. Instead, everything is worse than before.*

Why had he told her he was attracted to her? Especially after what she'd told him? She was right, it was poor judgment and nothing less than a slap in the face. Did he, in some dark part of his ego, think she'd come closer to faith because of *his* affections? He hated to admit himself capable of such arrogance. *I'm an absolute mess. Here I am, on the brink of the most important turning point in my life, I'm supposed to be leading a brilliant team, and I'm in shambles. Lord, where are You taking me? Where are You taking the show? Why won't You show me what to do?*

Drew stumbled on through his morning, not seeing Janet. He didn't expect to—if he never saw her again, he deserved no less. It killed him to know that last night's botched conversation would be their last. That was no way to end things between them.

The extra crews needed to film the final sequences would be flying in this afternoon. In two days the project would be wrapped up and he'd be on a plane to California to begin his new stint as the face of HomeBase and the network's new hit series. To a life he'd imagined for years, to a ministry bigger than he'd ever dreamed. Perhaps it was only to be expected that there would be some damage along the way. He just hated it to be Janet. It stung him to no end that *he'd* hurt her on top of what that Tony character had done to her. In his darker moments, Drew wondered if he'd been the final blow to her ever regaining her faith. Which, again, was an arrogant thought. It was God who gave people faith, who pulled souls toward Himself. Drew Downing was only a speck on the landscape.

Someone knocked on the bus door. When he

peered out the window he saw Dinah Hopkins, standing at the door with a final box of Muffin-novations.

"Hi," she said as he opened the door. "You got a minute?"

"For a lady bearing goodies, always. C'mon in."

Dinah set the box down on the table and took a minute to glance around the bus. "Nice digs." She ran a finger down the edge of the counter. "Look, Janet's a friend of mine. She's been a good friend since I moved here."

"She okay?"

"No, and I think you know why." Stuffing her hands into her back pockets, Dinah straightened up. "Don't give up on her. I know she's a tough case, but church hasn't exactly been a haven of rest for her. I think you might be the guy to get through. Really. So don't give up, okay?"

Drew leaned back against the cabinets. "I'm not sure she ever wants to talk to me again."

"I know, but you strike me as a persuasive kind of guy. I think maybe…" They were interrupted by Drew's cell phone buzzing on the table, but he didn't move to pick it up. Still, she nodded toward the phone. "You go ahead and take your call. I'm praying, I'm on your side, and I'll see you to-morrow." With that, Dinah turned on her heels and walked off the bus.

What was he supposed to do now? He couldn't change Janet's history with the church, and *Missionnovation* was just making things worse. His phone buzzed again. He wasn't surprised it was Charlie. Drew flipped open the phone and tucked the box of Muffinnovations into the pantry cabinet.

"What? You don't answer your phone anymore?"

"I was in the middle of an important conversation, Chuck."

"You know I pout when someone's more important than me," Charlie teased. "Are we on target?"

"It's tight, but we'll make it."

"The rest of the crew comes in tonight. Make this a good one, Drew. Our new friends will be watching."

Drew stared at the church lawn visible out the bus windows. It was coming together gloriously. The site swarmed with volunteers working toward the final deadline. "Gotcha."

"You okay with those papers I sent out? Legal's been through them and we're all ready to go."

"Send out the originals for me to sign. We're ready."

"Actually," Charlie replied, "that's one of the reasons why I called. We're going to do a signing ceremony with some network folks and some HomeBase brass the day after the shareholders' meeting. Turn it into a press conference. Okay by you?"

"Why not? But can we fly Kevin, Annie, Mike and Jeremy out for the signing thing? We should have the whole design team there. They deserve the limelight, too."

Drew heard Charlie punching calculator buttons, probably factoring in the cost of four additional airfares. "I think I can make that happen. And they like Kevin and the gang as much as they like you."

"That's why I like you, Charlie, you make it happen."

Drew hung up and returned to his previous worry. He wasn't sure he could set things straight with Janet, but based on Dinah's exhortations, maybe he needed to keep trying. This had become about something bigger than roofs or watering cans.

As he turned toward Bishop Hardware, he met Kevin venturing up the street on his crutches. He was getting pretty good with those things. Some member of the design team had actually painted them with green-and-white stripes overnight, and Kevin had been hobbling around town and the church, showing them off.

"You weren't kidding about Janet Bishop. I just went over there to get a new pair of shears this morning and she about sheared my head off."

"Um, that's sort of my doing," Drew admitted.

"We had a bit of an argument last night…this morning." Maybe right now wasn't the time to go make peace with her.

Kevin kept walking, heading toward the church. "What's going on between you two? You haven't gotten *complicated* with her, have you?"

Drew gaped at him. "No. You know me better than that. I *hope* you know me better than that."

"Well, you've been acting all weird lately. Distracted. And you told me she caught your eye. I wouldn't have thought you'd go for that type, but then again…"

"Yeah," Drew turned, coming around in front of Kevin. "Tell me about the 'then again' part. I happen to know you've got a little 'then again' going on in your life."

Kevin stopped, looking shocked but also not hiding a grin. "You know?"

Drew started walking again. "You two are about as subtle as Mayor Epson. I wouldn't have thought you'd go for that type, but *then again*." He nudged Kevin's elbow just a bit. "Way to go, sport. Although I think you could have caught her attention without falling off the church roof."

Kevin's grin faded into a nervous glance. "You're…um…okay with this?"

"Yeah." Drew smiled. Kevin looked absolutely smitten. "I'm fine with it. Really. Just dial down the public affection until we're off the air, okay? I want to keep the attention where it belongs."

Kevin nudged him back as best he could while still maneuvering the crutches. "On you?"

"On the church and the preschool. By the way, what did you learn looking at those plans?"

"It's just like you said," Kevin replied. "If we had loads of time and money, and HomeBase weren't giving it to us for such a deal, we could do the roof with the other materials. And yes, we could go through the whole complicated process of putting the cistern thing underground, but all that'd take us an extra week, if not more. Plus we'd lose our watering can."

"But is it *better?*"

"Ideal, maybe yes, but it's not a question of better. But this isn't a perfect world, and we can't always go with the ideal installations. Not by the twentieth, that's for sure. Don't forget—both of those items are add-ons. We were doing them a favor."

"So I made the right call?"

"Yes. Look, Drew, it's not like you're sticking them with some inferior product because it's the HomeBase weekly special. The HomeBase stuff is new, but it's quality, and as good as the stuff we were planning to use before. Besides, they'd never have been able to afford either without us." Kevin stopped walking for a moment and looked at him.

"You done good, rest easy. Janet will calm down one of these days, and if she doesn't, you'll be long gone anyhow."

Drew rolled his eyes. "Nice Christian attitude."

"I'm wounded and I've been up for thirty hours. This is as nice as I get."

Before Drew knew it, the afternoon was gone and it was time to get ready for the last prayer service. The final evening was always the best, and this one was no exception. It drew the largest crowd yet, with an excitement that could have powered the floodlights clear through the end of the week. Drew felt his energy return as the team and the dozens upon dozens of volunteers began to gear up for the final taping and handing over of the keys. Mayor Epson even led the crowd in a hymn, his booming baritone thundering over the crowd with characteristic importance. He was a textbook "octopus", wanting to be part of every aspect of *Missionnovation*'s final days. Even though they usually handed the keys over to the pastor on the final day, Howard insisted Drew hand the keys to *him*, and *he* would hand the keys to Pastor Anderson. And it was a giant, key-to-the-city kind of key Howard had made, rather than the ordinary *Missionnovation* key chain Drew normally used.

To Drew's great satisfaction, Annie led the meeting's final prayer. Without notes, on stage and over the microphone. And, just as suspected, she was fabulous. Kevin had heaped such encouragement on her in the last day that Annie didn't stand a chance of sinking back into the sidelines. Surprising as it was, Kevin really did bring out the best in her.

Equally as surprising, Annie brought out the best in Kevin. Even with one foot propped up, he displayed guitar skills Drew didn't know he had. More than once, Drew backed off and let Kevin take the lead. Those two really had come into their own this season. *You've given me an amazing team, Lord. They're ready to take* Missionnovation *to the next level. You've blessed them—and me— beyond measure.* When Janet's mother led a prayer of thanksgiving for all the workers who'd made the project a reality, Drew joined in with a heart full of gratitude.

None of that stopped him from scanning the audience for a certain set of brown eyes.

He knew she wouldn't be there. He knew he'd probably not get the chance to say goodbye, nor did he think forcing one would do anyone any good. She had too much history to see the situation objectively, and he didn't think one more conversation would change that. Drew wasn't a man given to many regrets, but as he packed up the sound equipment that night, he had the sinking feeling that Janet Bishop would always be one of them. *Call her back to Yourself, Lord,* Drew prayed. *Redeem what that man took. Send someone to heal her. I understand it can't be me.*

The great Drew Downing really had finally met the one wall he couldn't tear down.

Chapter Twenty-Three

The state fair had nothing on Middleburg today. Janet sat on the hood of her Jeep and watched the crowd cheer as Howard Epson handed a giant green-and-white key to Pastor Anderson. There were twice as many cameras as usual, and that wasn't counting the four local television crews. The church lawn was a sea of green T-shirts and white baseball hats. Janet imagined she was one of the only people in town not standing on the church lawn. Half the businesses shut down for the day, and Howard even got in a fight with the school board over whether or not to let classes out early.

She couldn't bring herself to go, even though she ought to have been there—she was, after all, a vendor and a participant. It had cut too close, however, become too personal, to allow her to stand among the happy crowd and cheer. It felt safer to watch from a distance.

Camera crews followed Drew and the others around to the west side of the church, and Janet was certain she could hear the "oohs" and "aahs" as they unveiled God's watering can and the adorable preschool garden. The garden she couldn't go back to just yet.

The next day, every time a plane flew overhead, Janet looked up, wondering if Drew and the rest of the team were on their way to the legendary meeting Annie had told her about. Big things were about to happen for them. She really did wish them well. They were mostly good people doing good things. *Missionnovation* had just become about too many things for her, and she needed distance. From them. From him. The preschool was open and running now, and things would be edging their way back to normal over the next week.

Janet hadn't even realized she'd been standing staring at the extra cans of Preservation Task Force Approved Church Door Blue paint until Vern came up and stood beside her. For a moment he just let out a deep breath and thrust his hands deeper into his overalls pockets. Then he looked at her and said, "You don't think it's perfect, do you? And that makes you mad."

"Well, yes." It was that, but it was more than

that—only she wasn't ready to talk about the rest of it. She put down the can. "They let us down, Vern. They came in here all promises and big talk and…they let us down."

Vern looked around the empty store. "Let who down? I don't see anyone else looking unhappy. Middleburg got a new preschool just like they promised. Pastor Anderson tells me he got a whole bunch of stuff he didn't need even before the storm. Prayers got answered."

"They installed the roof and cistern wrong. There was a right way to do it and they took short-cuts instead."

"That's just how *you* choose to see it. Janny-bean, you got this perfect world in your head. Some idea of how the world should be, and it burns you up when the world don't agree. I ain't never met a perfect person. Or a perfect plan, a perfect house, a perfect marriage or a perfect church. If life and people were perfect, Jesus'd be out of a job, don't you think?"

"He let me down, Vern. He was supposed to be the real deal, this guy who cared about doing the right thing, and he took shortcuts."

"I ain't so sure I share your opinion, but okay, what if he did? What if Drew Downing messed up on that tank? What if the roof leaks? Does that take away everything else—every good thing—he did?"

"It does to me."

Vern heaved a sigh that broadcast his disappointment and walked back down the aisle.

"Mr. Missionnovation himself, Drew Downing!" The announcer's voice boomed over the loudspeakers in the hotel banquet room. The lights came up as a huge screen that had just played segments of half a dozen *Missionnovation* programs retracted into the ceiling. Drew walked over to the HomeBase CEO and shook his hand.

"This is the beginning of a great partnership," the man said into the podium microphone. "A whole host of products and promotions lay ahead as HomeBase takes the warmth and values of *Missionnovation* to prime-time network television."

True to their word, HomeBase hadn't edited any of the faith out of the *Missionnovation* segments they aired to their shareholders. Granted, Drew didn't much care for America's families of faith being referred to as a "rich, untapped market segment," but if it got the word out undiluted and expanded, he didn't see how he could complain. Eyes lit up around the room as Drew talked about his vision for an expanded *Missionnovation*. People were getting it. They were buying into the show's concept. A few people even told him afterward that they'd started shopping at HomeBase because of its willingness to put its weight behind a faith-based show like *Missionnovation.* Drew had the overwhelming sensation that God had big plans for *Missionnovation,* and it was his job to hold on tight and take the wild ride.

Charlie was positively beaming when they met up at the end of the session. "Can you believe it? Did you ever imagine we'd be here? Doing this? On this scale?" Charlie slapped Drew on the back and shook his hand. "After tomorrow, the whole country will know what *Missionnovation* is and what it stands for."

"I can't wait for the rest of the team to get here. I want them to see this."

"They get in at ten o'clock tonight. I had my assistant check in with Kevin earlier, and everything is wrapping up nicely in Kentucky." Charlie guided Drew through the sea of new fans toward the table where a lot of important looking people sat starting in on their dessert. With a sad twinge, Drew noted that the plates were filled with very ordinary looking chocolate sheet cake—a serious let-down from the delicious originality of Milk and Cookies Pie and Muffinnovations. "The editor says the tapes look great," Charlie continued. "We should have a rough edit of the final episode within a few weeks. I think we'll even have a thirty-second segment talking about the new expanded season and the HomeBase sponsorship. Gentlemen, we're one our way to an amazing success."

The rest of the day was a blur of handshakes, photographs, planning meetings and congratulations. He was introduced to loads of people, but he didn't really meet any of them. They were a sea of nameless faces, not unique individuals. When he finally sank onto his hotel bed at eleven o'clock that night, Drew thought he couldn't keep his eyes open one minute longer. Which was funny, because jam-packed days usually left Drew feeling charged-up, not wiped out. He was glad of the chance to get his first full night's sleep in weeks.

Glad, that is, until a knock came on his door. Drew dragged himself off the bed and stumbled wearily to the peephole. Kevin stood on the other side of the door, flanked by his green-and-white crutches.

Drew pulled the door open. "You made it. Everybody get settled in okay?"

"Best flight ever. I love it that you get to board first if you're on crutches." Kevin grinned. "They put me in first class because my leg wouldn't bend enough to fit in coach. Outstanding."

Drew laughed. "I'm glad. Who knows, they may fly us first class from here on in when we're not on our spiffy new busses."

"Whatever. I'm beat. I'm gonna sink like a stone onto that big fluffy bed and wake up a new man." His voice took on a teasing tone as he fumbled to pull an envelope from his back pocket. "First, though, I've got to deliver a little message someone left for you." To Drew's surprise, Kevin waved a Bishop Hardware envelope in the air. "Seems like someone finally came around. That's my Drew. Wins 'em over every time." Kevin pointed at Drew with a smirk. "I gotta admit, I wasn't sure you were going to pull this one off."

Drew took the envelope, speechless. He was glad Kevin gathered his crutches and hobbled off down the hall without waiting for him to open the message from Janet. He suspected it was of a private nature, anyway. *Thanks, God. I didn't want it to end the way it did.*

Drew sank slowly down onto a chair and slid his finger under the envelope seal. Nothing fancy, just plain white paper with no-nonsense lettering in the corner. No spiffy colors or catchy logos—pure Janet Bishop practicality.

His heart sank as the contents of the envelope fluttered out onto the floor.

A single piece of paper. A check.

She'd filled out the check he gave her on his first day. The blank check he'd given her to fund repairs if she ever felt *Missionnovation* hadn't lived up to its promise of quality work.

She'd filled it out for the amount of the original roofing supplies and returned it to him, uncashed.

Chapter Twenty-Four

It can't be helped. I did everything I could do, didn't I, Lord? We did a fine job for Middleburg. We went beyond what they requested. It's not my fault, is it, Lord? Drew fingered his way through the Gospel of Matthew, his favorite, looking for something to speak to his heavy spirit. He read through the parable of the seeds. Janet was "scorched earth" right now, any seed that was sown wouldn't take root. He'd always known he couldn't bring everyone around, but he couldn't get past his frustration over Janet. Every soul mattered to him, but Janet was different. And it wasn't even just about faith. He couldn't shake the notion he'd let her down professionally. Personally.

Feeling no reassurance, Drew read further, looking for something to allow him to move on. He read over the parable of the lost sheep, sympathizing with the man Jesus said would leave his ninety-nine sheep to go find the one lost lamb. But he couldn't find Janet—that was Jesus's job. *Go after her, Lord,* he prayed. *Be relentless. Don't let her go.*

Janet made it crystal clear she felt as if she'd been wronged. He didn't agree with her, but he knew that logic didn't necessarily explain how someone *felt.* So Drew wandered into Luke's gospel, looking for what Jesus did with people who'd been wronged. When he hit upon the Pharisee asking Jesus "Who is my neighbor?" in Chapter ten, he halted. Wasn't he, in fact, asking himself the same thing? If Janet's wounds were his responsibility to heal? He sat up in bed and read the parable of the Good Samaritan further.

No one *had* to help the man who'd been robbed. They were visitors—bystanders who happened upon the victim. And compassion did require you to help someone like that. While no one else had, the Good Samaritan did a whole lot of good on behalf of the victimized man in the story.

But he didn't stop there. He went way beyond the expected. Beyond what he *ought* to do into all he knew he *could* do. Beyond just his obligation and into the depth of his capacity.

Drew stilled, knowing he'd hit upon the passage God intended him to find. He was wide awake, even at three in the morning.

Missionnovation had done its job. They'd given Middleburg more than it asked for. Sowed all kinds of seed in that quaint little town. Pastor Anderson told him several stories of people whose faith had been strengthened by the work of *Missionnovation*. They'd not only repaired the preschool, they'd made dozens of improvements on the church itself. Howard Epson was so proud, Drew thought he'd explode before the day was over. They'd filmed a spectacular final episode, wrapping up one season only to vault into a new, expanded format. No one could fault him for the work he did. But deep inside, Drew knew he held the capacity to do more for one particular woman. Even if it meant going to extraordinary lengths.

It was no accident he'd given Janet that blank check. God had placed Janet in his life, and he in Janet's. Drew's constant ache for her was God telling him to make Janet's healing his problem, because perhaps God chose him to be the solution. Hadn't Dinah Hopkins told him as much? Yes, Janet's "repair" was something only God could accomplish, but Drew knew he was supposed to play a part in her healing. A big part. Because God had planted a caring for her in his heart that was stronger than he could ever hope to ignore.

And, truth be told, he was kidding himself to think that all of his unrest had solely been about

Janet. In reality, Janet's situation had only been the barometer for lots of things Drew had been sweeping under his own personal rug. *Missionnovation* was a different enterprise than when he started. He thought he'd wanted expansion, visibility, all the qualities of "bigger and better," but it wasn't what he really wanted.

He wanted what *Missionnovation* used to be. Middleburg was feeling too much like the last of its kind—like something he wasn't ready to let go. He thought it was simply projects *like* Middleburg, the face-to-face, get-to-know-you projects, but Drew realized it was Middleburg, itself. *Missionnovation* was moving on, but Drew knew he no longer wanted to move with it. The show had grown beyond his dreams, beyond what made him happy.

That didn't make it bad, it just made it time to say goodbye.

Drew dialed Charlie's cell phone as early as he dared. "Can't wait for the big day, huh?" Charlie yawned into the phone.

"We have to talk, Charlie. Now."

Charlie looked about as calm as one could expect under the circumstances—which wasn't calm at all. As a matter of fact, it was the closest thing to panic Drew had ever seen on the man's face.

"Let me get this straight," Charlie said, rubbing

his hands down his face as they sat in the hotel coffee shop with the smog-tinted Los Angeles sun just dawning over his shoulder. "You're leaving *Missionnovation?* For a *girl?*"

"She's not a *girl,*" Drew sighed. "In my experience women don't take nicely to being called girls. And it's not just about Janet. She just sort of brought everything to a head, that's all."

"I don't get it." Charlie stared at him, genuinely stumped. "Now, of all times, when we're about to go big—now you leave?"

"I think that's just it, Charlie. I thought I wanted *Missionnovation* to 'go big.' I understand all the reasons why it's a good thing. But for the first time since we started, I think I finally understand the difference between Drew Downing and Mr. Missionnovation. I want *Missionnovation* to go big. But *I* don't—all those trappings of a big show, none of that appeals to me. None of it feels right. My brain's been mud since we started this negotiation and I couldn't figure out why. It's because I've lost my bearings. I never wanted to be famous, I just wanted to help people fix stuff. Show them how the body of Christ helps each other out. And somehow, in a way I can't really explain yet, doing it on a big scale isn't what I'm supposed to be doing. It's not the crowds that jazz me, it's the one-on-one. Don't you get it? That's why I'm always fixated on the 'hostile' even though the whole crowd is cheering."

"Your timing is lousy."

Drew managed a thin smile. "It's not my timing. Actually, I think I'm a little late on the uptake. I think God's been shouting in my ear for weeks now and it took Janet Bishop to shake me up enough to hear Him. This is something I have to do."

Charlie still looked forlorn.

"Look, I think you had the notion right—that it was time for my role in *Missionnovation* to change. You just didn't realize that *launching Missionnovation* was my thing. Tinkering with it until she was strong enough to fly on her own. Kevin and Annie and the rest of them, they're ready. I got them ready, and I've been so blessed by it. They'll be great. This isn't going to fall around your ankles. It's really going to take off because now you'll have the people God intends taking it from here."

"You sure know how to test a guy's faith." Charlie gulped his coffee—his fourth cup. "I'm not sure I can pull this off."

"I am," Drew replied, meaning every word of it. "You're the guy who makes things happen. And I know this is what's supposed to happen. I've known it since the minute I figured it out, and it feels right. Really right. You have to know I'm sure or I would never get you out of bed at this hideous hour."

"It's dawn," Charlie said, cringing. "I don't do dawn."

"It's one of the most amazing times in Kentucky. You should see the mist, Charlie. It takes your breath away."

"Man," said Charlie, narrowing his eyes. "You do have it bad."

Drew grinned. He did, didn't he?

"Start praying, Downing. And get everyone you know on their knees. It's gonna take God in all His might to pull today off."

"Welcome to my world, Chuck. If God in all His might didn't show up every day, I'd have been sunk three years ago."

Janet found her mom in her garage, putting away gardening supplies for the winter. As it had always been, the Bishop garage was tidy—swept, organized, with a place for everything and everything in its place. Her dad used to joke that even the garden hoses wouldn't dare kink or wind in the wrong direction when Bebe Bishop was in charge. Her mom pulled off a pair of work gloves and straightened when Janet came up the driveway. "Well hello, dear. Nice to have everything back to normal up at the shop?"

That was the question of the hour, wasn't it? Was it nice? And was everything back to normal?

No, and no.

No matter how she tried to deny it, Drew Downing had left things too quiet at the shop and too stormy in her soul.

"Got a minute? Can I talk to you about something?" Janet said as casually as she could. She tried to make it sound trivial, but moms have a radar about that sort of thing, and her mother dropped the gloves immediately and gestured toward the back door.

She poured two glasses of iced tea—Bebe drank iced tea year round, preferring cold drinks to hot for as long as Janet could remember—and sat down at the kitchen table. "What's on your mind?"

"How'd you marry Dad?" She could have picked a more subtle start, but couldn't think of one.

A smile washed over her mother's face. "Well, there was a minister, and he said the usual things, and we said the usual things, and we were married."

Janet rolled her eyes. Couldn't her mother see she was trying to have a serious conversation? "I mean how'd you *decide* to marry Dad?"

Bebe sat back. "That's a mite more complicated. Then again, not really. I loved him, and you don't really decide something like that. It just sort of happens." She stirred her tea. "But I did have to decide to marry him. And that wasn't quite as easy. I knew I could when I wanted a *life with him* more than I cared about the challenges of *living with him.* No one gets married without a few doubts." She looked at Janet. "Why the sudden questions?"

"Vern and I argued because I'm mad at Drew Downing. You know I think *Missionnovation* made mistakes over at MCC. Vern told me to hush up and be grateful, to accept an imperfect world with imperfect people." Janet ran her finger around the top of her iced tea glass, not feeling very thirsty. "He said something about how even Dad was imperfect, and to ask you about it."

"He and your dad were in the middle of a big fight when your father died. Actually, he and your dad fought a lot."

Dad and Vern? Fighting? They somehow managed to keep her from seeing it. "What could those two fight about?"

"Oh, you'd be surprised. Your dad had a stubborn streak a mile wide. But you wouldn't know anything about bein' stubborn, or insisting on your own way, now would you?"

Janet let that go without a reply. She knew perfectly well where her stubborn steak came from.

"I'm not saying your dad wasn't a wonderful man—he was." Her mother's eyes strayed to the dark blue Bishop Hardware jacket hung on a peg by the back door. "But Vern is right, and no one's perfect. You know your dad had one way of doing things—his way. He had blinders on as to anyone else's ideas, no matter how fine they might be." Janet recalled the dozens of arguments she'd had with her dad over how to run the store. "Before you took over, Vern had a front row seat to most of it. People make mistakes when they won't take advantage of good advice and only see their own way on things."

Janet toyed with the ice cubes in her glass. "I know Dad could be a tough boss. I still don't see what that's got to do with *Missionnovation.*"

"Well, like I said, I did think about your dad's faults before I said yes to his proposal. I had to decide if I liked the good things of a life with him more than I wanted to get my own way most of the time. I loved your dad to pieces, but he was a bit of a schemer, and that didn't always sit well with me. I had to take the good with the bad."

"Dad? Scheming?"

Bebe chuckled. "Well, I suppose it looked more like planning to you. You two are so alike in lots of ways. But Dad had been a schemer when he was younger. That's why he was so angry about what happened with Tony. Saw his former self in that boy. And it made him furious." She looked at Janet tenderly. "It broke his heart to see what happened to you. I always hoped, for your sake, that with some mercy Tony would wise up and turn his life around. 'Course, I was wrong. I never thought you'd be so hurt by all of it for so long." She stared down at her hands. "I would've come down like the wrath of God on that boy if I'd known he was gonna destroy your faith. I just kept thinking of Jacob, how scheming he was, but how God turned him around to be such a man of faith." She looked up at Janet. "I wanted Tony to be like your dad, but he wasn't, and that's my mistake."

"Tony was never Jacob," Janet said bitterly. "And Tony was never Dad. He had us all fooled."

Her mother leaned in and grabbed Janet's arm across the table. "I know. Mercy, how I know that now. But Jannybean, the whole world ain't like that. I wish I could make you see that. You fell for a bad man, and I'm sorry every day for what it did to you. But I think the right man is out there, waiting for you to come round, just like God is."

Chapter Twenty-Five

Janet expected the conversation with her mom to make things clearer, but it didn't. She bumped around the house all evening, unable to work on birdhouses, unable to find anything to do or eat or read and she certainly didn't want to watch television. She wandered the house, restless, until she ended back at her workbench, trying to sketch ideas for new birdhouses. Every attempt ended up wadded in the trash—nothing seemed to work for her tonight.

Her eyes landed on the Bible where it had fallen off her workbench, waiting to be picked up. The Bible had its share of imperfect people with plans gone wrong. Jacob, for example. She also remembered Jacob as quite the schemer, and something about him meeting his future wife Rachel at a well.

A well. A cistern, if you will.

Her faith was like this Bible. It was waiting, but she'd have to make the step of picking it up. It had never changed—it was still the same Bible that had guided her through such leaps of faith at church—only her distance from it had changed.

She picked up the book and opened to Genesis, thumbing through the pages until she caught sight of Jacob's name. She wandered back until she found the twenty-fifth chapter where Jacob and Esau began their adventures in life. The stories were filled with deceit, plans gone sour, bad advice and all kinds of wrong turns. As she read them, the tales became not so much about a man gone wrong as they were about a God determined to set things right. God loved Jacob, warts and all. Jacob's faults didn't make God any less powerful or less righteous. God was God all along—He only seemed to fade when you stopped looking at Him.

She had let Tony stand in for God. Let Tony's shadow block out anything Drew or *Missionnovation* may have shown her about God. Let Tony's sins define church and faith when it was God who should define her church and her faith. A God who hadn't moved His eyes off her no matter how long it had been since she looked at Him.

Janet poured on through Jacob's life until she hit the story of Joseph. She laughed when she read about holes in the ground causing more trouble—Joseph's brothers threw him in a pit to get rid of him. Two thousand years later, and holes in the ground were still wreaking havoc on relationships. As she read of Joseph's prayers in prison—a man who definitely understood what it was like to be hurt by someone else's deceit—an understanding seemed to dawn. Joseph didn't ignore Potiphar's wife's crimes. Her lie about his conduct landed him in jail. Yet, Joseph didn't let that scheming woman define his God. Joseph allowed his faith to stake a claim in God's bigger plan for his life, even when all he could see were dire consequences.

If Joseph—who'd endured far more than a broken heart—could find a way to keep faith in God, then maybe Janet could find a way to return to faith.

I don't know how, she offered up the fragile prayer. *But You do. You can chart my path back. You already have, haven't You? It's begun already. That big green bus really was a blessing, I was just too hurt to see it. Too caught up in the imperfections to see all the good things You brought to Middleburg through it.*

She remembered now the verse her mother would quote to her when she became especially bitter about what had happened with Tony. "I will repay you for the years the locust have eaten." She had lost years. More importantly, she'd lost hope. Perhaps it was time she asked God to restore both. *Can I come back, Lord? Can You take away the bitterness? I don't want to let Tony steal any more than he already has.* Janet picked up the Bible and took it to her couch, looking up "locusts" in the concordance in the back to see if she could find the verse.

When she found it in Joel, it was as if the verses jumped off the page to speak to her. The way they once had.

"Even now," declares the LORD, *"return to me with all your heart, with fasting and weeping and mourning. Rend your heart and not your garments. Return to the LORD your God, for He is gracious and compassionate, slow to anger and abounding in love, and He relents from sending calamity."*

Wasn't that exactly what she'd feared? That He'd sent calamity in the form of Drew Downing? She could come back. In fact, God had been waiting, patiently, for her return. And she knew, even if she knew nothing else, that the door of Middleburg Community Church would always be open once she found her way there.

She decided, just then, that her next birdhouse would be shaped like a wishing well. Not exactly a house, but then again, maybe it was time for holes in the ground to get a new reputation.

* * *

Drew sat at an enormous black conference table between a line of network high-ups and several HomeBase executives.

Charlie, seated next to Drew, looked like he'd just run a marathon. Kevin and Annie were on the sidelines of the room, holding hands and looking nervous. Jeremy looked as if he hadn't decided how this was going to affect his precious career path. Mike hadn't even flinched.

"*Missionnovation* will move forward in exciting new directions with Kevin and Annie at the helm. It's time for me to step aside and move on to other projects." Drew caught Charlie's glance out of the corner of his eye. "I'll stay on board through the Christmas special and remain as an executive consultant to the production team. I'll do whatever limited appearances HomeBase deems necessary, and oversee whatever's needed to let these folks take *Missionnovation* into its new format." At that, all eyes turned to the quartet on the sidelines. They were ready to take the spotlight. Drew knew it, and they were beginning to see it as well.

Chapter Twenty-Six

Janet hung a new beach-shack birdhouse in the window of Bishop Hardware. The week before, she'd presented Pastor Anderson with a new bird-house—the wishing well birdhouse—for the church lawn. He'd been delighted to accept a second birdhouse, but he made sure Janet knew he was far more delighted to have her in church again.

Her return to church was not the usual "come back to Jesus" dramatic moment. As a matter of fact, Pastor Anderson joked with her about having the most unusual return to faith of his career. It had started with daily inspections of the new roof. Excessive, yes, but Janet couldn't shake the constant need to look it over, watch it, guard it.

As she made those visits, she and Pastor Anderson began to talk about all that had happened, about God, even about Drew. Then it didn't seem like such a big leap to stay for a Wednesday night service. Then a Sunday morning. Then every Sunday morning.

The original church replica birdhouse now sat on a post right next to the giant watering can Janet still couldn't bring herself to like. Everyone thought it was the cleverest thing they'd ever seen, and while she stopped saying it, she still believed it belonged underground. She'd made a little bargain with herself about that tank—she'd keep her mouth shut through the winter. If it survived the freeze without problems, she'd revise her opinion. If it broke or heaved or did anything of that sort, she'd allow herself the luxury of a loud, long, "I told you so."

Vern was late to work this morning. Granted, business wasn't exactly booming this late into October, but it still wasn't like Vern to ever show up anything less than five minutes early. With a tug of alarm, she hoped nothing had happened to that dear old man. He lived alone, and he was getting on in years.

She was just getting ready to call Vern's house when an unfamiliar car pulled up and parked right outside the shop windows. Vern got out of the passenger side, waving to whomever was inside. He walked into work with a wide smile, whistling besides.

"Who drove you to work, old man?" Janet

snapped the ladder shut and pulled it back into the shop.

"Wouldn't you like to know, missy?" Vern practically winked. *Winked*. Something was definitely up. "I'm just gonna head on back into the stockroom and tidy up a bit."

Vern? Tidy up? Not in a million years. "What's going on?"

"Oh, nothin'."

Shaking her head, Janet headed to the back of the store to put the ladder away. A minute or two later she heard someone call out, "Well hello again and how are ya, Middleburg?"

She knew that voice. Janet turned to find Drew Downing standing in the paint aisle. Drew Downing, standing with his hands in his pockets and a gigawatt grin on his face, in her paint aisle.

"I'm here to check on a certain roof. The frost'll set in soon, and I want to make sure there'll be no leaks. So I need a ladder." He walked toward her, and Janet thought the paint aisle might just blow away to bits behind her.

Janet found her voice. "You're here?" she gulped out.

"I took a few days off. Actually, I took most of next season off. I'm still there, sort of, but it's going to be Kevin and Annie's thing now. They make a really good team."

She'd heard things about how Drew Downing was changing his role in *Missionnovation*. She had tried not to think about what that might mean. Now, she didn't know what to think. Thoughts of surprise and suspicion and delight were colliding so fast in her head she couldn't sort them out. "Why are you here?"

"Like I said, I came back to check on the roof."

"Why'd you come back to check on the roof?" It wasn't fair. He looked even better than he did before. Less theatric, which made him all the more handsome somehow. Janet's insides were doing jumping jacks, and she found a broom at the corner of the aisle and held on to it for support.

"Because that's the kind of man I want to be. But, you know, I'd lost sight of that for a while." Drew fished a slip of paper out of his pocket. It was the check she'd sent back to him through Kevin. She cringed, thinking what a mean gesture that had been. More than once she'd tamped down the urge to call him and take it back, especially when the roof showed no signs of problems. "I needed a wake-up call, Janet. I was turning into someone I didn't recognize, and it took you to show it to me. So I'm back to check on your roof. And I'm going to keep checking on it all winter. And I'm going to fix anything that goes wrong." He raised an eyebrow, "But I'm here to tell you,

I don't think anything is going to go wrong. Your church got a good roof. I'm just here to stand by my work." A grin swept across his face. "And a few other things. So, you got any ladders?"

Janet nodded and stumbled toward the aisle where ladders were kept. "We've got ladders over at the church. You won't need one of your own."

He stopped walking, and a warm look lit up his face. "We?"

Even though part of her had yearned to call or write Drew and tell him she'd found her way back to the church, she never could find the nerve. Now that he was standing here, the words eluded her. "You…um…you might say I finally came around. Isn't that how you always put it?"

She couldn't describe the expression on his face. Part surprise, a hint of wonder, genuinely happy, and something she wasn't sure she was ready to call affection. Which was a lie—she was more than ready to call it affection. His eyes melted her composure and did something warm and wonderful to her soul. "I don't suppose you've got a minute to walk over and show me how you think the roof is holding up?"

Janet could think of nothing better she'd like to do at the moment. Smiling—probably grinning like a fool, she thought to herself—she managed to say, "I think I can find the time."

* * *

She was even more beautiful than he remembered. She'd changed. Even if she hadn't told him she'd made peace with the church, he'd have known it by the way she looked. There was an inner quietness about her that had always been there before, but seemed to be in full bloom now. Something spacious in her eyes. He knew, as he followed her around the church, poking into crawl spaces and looking at gutter fastenings, that he'd always been in love with her. Maybe even from the first day, but now, as she stood close to him looking up at the steeple flashings, he could barely hear the words she was saying for the thumping of his heart in his ears. This was the stuff of high school crushes, not a grown man renewing his professional integrity. Go slow, he kept telling himself, even though he counted no less that six times he could have pulled her to him and kissed her if it wasn't such a dangerous idea. He'd never been a patient man, and now he seemed drowning in impatience.

"So," she was saying as they walked under a tree in the church's front yard, "I'm watching this section over here because it gets so much moisture." She was blushing. A rosy glow he felt tingle through his fingertips and made him itch to brush his hand against her cheek.

"You're right, that will be the spot trouble shows up. *If* it shows up. But I don't think it will." He caught sight of a birdhouse hanging from the tree branches. It was a charming wishing well. He knew instantly it was hers, and something uncurled deep in his chest. "This yours?" he could barely gulp out.

She nodded.

"It's wonderful." It was just a birdhouse, but at that moment Drew thought it the most beautiful thing he'd ever seen. Well, maybe second most.

"Drew," she said quietly, "I'm really glad you came back."

He looked down for a long moment, and when he looked up, Drew felt his restraint puddle out through the soles of his shoes. *Oh, Lord, You're going to have to help me here. I'm a goner.* "I had to come back," he admitted, feeling like he was admitting far more. "For me. For you."

With a surety he never expected, Janet leaned in and kissed him. A gentle, feather-light kiss that washed over him like a blinding light. The perfect stillness of it startled him. It was as if all the frenetic energy, all the business of his life had rushed to this single moment. The place where everything came together. *Her. Here.* He pulled his hands up to cup her face—as much to hold himself upright as to give in to the urge to touch her. The indescribable softness of her took his breath away. He loved her. It didn't solve everything, and it didn't need to. He'd take it however slow it needed to go from here, even if it near killed him. She was worth it.

She always had been.

Chapter Twenty-Seven

The roof was holding up beautifully. Drew was back for his second monthly check-in, and Janet knew she'd have to concede her point when he showed up this afternoon. His roof installation had been a good choice. She was ready to admit that now. She was ready to admit a few other things—like the fact that she was head-over-heels in love with Mr. Missionnovation himself, the last person she'd expect, Drew Downing.

Granted, he was making it hard not to fall for him. Drew Downing's full-force charm was a powerful thing. Sure, the daily e-mails were amusing. He'd regale her with tales of Kevin and Annie's doe-eyed romance and how it drove Mike and Jeremy crazy. He'd complain about the food now that every meal on earth seemed to pale next to something from Gina Deacon's Grill. Most of all, he'd tell her all about his plans to come to Middleburg once he'd finished his final tasks with the show. How they'd walk to church together or go get cookies from Dinah's bakery on Thursday mornings. How he'd court her like a true Kentucky son—even though she was pretty sure there wasn't an ounce of rural manner anywhere in that man. Which was fine, because she loved Drew just the way God made him.

She'd been fussing around the store all afternoon, jumping every time the bell over the store's front door jingled. Each time Vern would catch her eye with a mile-wide smile. You'd think he'd introduced her to Drew, the way Vern took credit for their relationship. He seemed to enjoy it so much, however, that she couldn't begrudge him whatever role he'd imagined in her happiness. Because that's really what it was—Vern was just glad to see her happy.

And she was. Some days it baffled Janet why it had taken her so long to come around to her faith again. It seemed silly now, to hold so deep a grudge for so long. She'd denied herself years of peace just to hang on to a hurt—a deep hurt, granted, but one that Jesus was more than ready to heal once she'd turned back to her faith. Janet used to wonder what she'd do if she ever saw Tony again. Now, it hardly seemed worth a thought. After so much time looking back, she had rediscovered the joy of looking forward.

She'd bought a silver filigree necklace and earring set—fussy, completely non-sensible things that caught her eye one afternoon at Emily Montague's West of Paris shop—and she smiled at her reflection in the store window. She'd bought some richly scented lotion, too— so uncharacteristic it made Emily grin like a cat and make some remark about "the power of love to make a woman glow." Emily ought to know, she and Gil were getting married in just a few months on Valentine's Day, and Emily had already made Janet promise to bring Drew to the wedding.

It seemed like hours before Drew's dark green truck would pull up in front of the store and take her to lunch. Which was why she was completely surprised to see him chug up the street in a small yellow backhoe. Construction equipment didn't seem like the ideal lunch-date vehicle—even for a guy as unpredictable as Drew Downing.

"Hello there, beautiful!" he called as the small-scale digging vehicle groaned to a stop beside the curb. He'd started calling her "beautiful" during his last visit and hadn't stopped since. It still made her blush. "Like my ride?"

"It's a backhoe, Drew."

"Yep. A little smaller than most, but just the right size for the job I have in mind." He pulled a picnic basket out from behind him on the seat. "I stopped at Deacon's on the way over for our lunch. I didn't forget I promised you lunch."

Janet couldn't help but laugh. "You drove to The Grill in that?"

"I drew a crowd."

"I'm not surprised." Janet surveyed the bright yellow machine. "It's kind of cute—in a construction-ish, technical kind of way."

"I'm going to dig me a hole." He affected a Kentucky twang with disastrous results that would make even Dinah groan.

As if that weren't obvious. "No kidding?"

"Really. Hop on. I'll give you a lift over to the church."

There hardly seemed room to fit two people on the backhoe's little metal seat, but when Drew wrapped his arm around her and pulled her close, she wondered if that wasn't what Drew had planned all along. It took nearly ten minutes to go the short trip, chugging along slowly as they were. "What are we going to dig?"

Drew's smile was warm and broad. "We're going to bury a water tank. I spent the last two weeks talking with the guy who builds these things, and I've decided you were right. It goes underground. So, we're going to dig the hole and put it where it belongs."

Not that it was ever about the tank, but if Janet hadn't known she loved him before, she was doubly sure of it now. She kissed his cheek tenderly.

"Whoa, woman, I need to keep my eyes on the road," he chuckled.

"You are the real deal, just like you said. And I love you for it." She'd planned to be more deliberate in how she told him, to make a big moment of it, but somehow now seemed the perfect time.

The backhoe stopped and Drew took his hands off the steering wheel to touch her face. He didn't say anything for the longest moment, only looked at her with such heart-stopping intensity that she thought she would burst. Then he leaned in and kissed her so powerfully that someone honked as they drove past them on the road.

"We're a moving violation," he joked as he pulled his attention back to the idling machine. "And I'm loving every minute of it." He pulled her into the crook of his shoulder and she snuggled up against him. Romance on a crawling backhoe. That was something only Drew Downing could pull off. "I've loved you from the first minute, you know that?" he said, sneaking a kiss into her hair while attempting to keep his eyes responsibly on the road. "I was just too busy fixing things to stop and fix myself."

He kissed her again, longer this time, when the backhoe pulled up around the back of the church. She'd known it would be like this, but it still felt surprising and wonderful. "There was something I was going to tell you today, even before you announced your little project here."

"You've already told me everything I wanted to hear."

"No, there's more." She couldn't help but grin.

"And what's that?" he asked as he pulled the picnic basket off the back of the machine.

"I think the roof is sound. You made the right choice and I was wrong."

He looked up at her. "I'm glad to hear that. I never pulled anything over on you or the church, Janet, ever. The only person I ever fooled in Middleburg was me." He walked toward her and reached for her hand. "*Missionnovation* was great, but all I ever wanted was to be the real deal. I didn't realize they might be two different things until I came here."

An hour later, Drew and Janet shared a picnic lunch beside a large hole in the preschool garden. "Jacob, hmm?"

Janet repeated to him the story of how she'd picked up her Bible the first time, and her roof-inspection path back to faith. She'd told him the story on his last visit, but he asked to hear it again.

"Well, Jacob and a whole lot of other scripture since. Dinah's asked me to be part of her Bible study group. I'm glad to be finding my way back. Slowly, but you know me, I like to take my time and make sure I do things right."

"I like that about you. Thoughtful, deliberate, non-impulsive. Fine qualities." He held her eyes for a moment longer before picking up a thermos of coffee Gina had packed for them. Along with a healthy supply of chocolate chip cookies. Drew closed his eyes for a moment and lifted his head toward the strong November sunshine. "Thank you, Lord, for bringing me here, for bringing me home. For bringing me," he turned his head and looked into her eyes, "to you." Slowly, without leaving her gaze and with the closest thing Drew Downing might ever show to patience, he kissed her hand. "I do love you."

Three weeks later, just before the holidays set in, Drew set the last stone in place on a charming wishing well in the corner of the preschool garden. The well sat on the ground that covered a tank. A tank Drew Downing buried to heal the woman he loved, and unearth the man he really was.

And it was…perfect.

* * * * *

Dear Reader,

Makeovers *look* fun. Lots of times, however, such "renovations" uncover as many problems as they solve. Painfully, tearing down walls always reveals what's behind them—but the results are often worth the hassles.

Drew and Janet annoy each other, but they bring out precious blessings in each other, too. People who "get under our skin" get there for a reason— even if we can't always see it at first. God sends us challenging relationships because we grow so much from them. I hope *Bluegrass Courtship* allows you to look at such trials with new eyes.

If this is your first visit to Middleburg, I hope you'll go back and find *Bluegrass Hero* to meet other Middleburg neighbors. Get ready for a third visit in *Bluegrass Blessings* later this year. Blessings to each of you. Write me anytime at www.allie-pleiter.com, or P.O. Box 7026, Villa Park, IL 60181.

Allie Pleiter

QUESTIONS FOR DISCUSSION

1. What if *Missionnovation* came to your home or church? What would you overhaul and why?

2. Do you know (or are you) an "octopus"? What motivates that behavior?

3. Why is fraud like Tony's so damaging? How can God help people and communities heal from wounds like that?

4. Do you have something—like Janet's sawdust— that brings back strong memories? What is it and why does it evoke such powerful emotions?

5. What's your opinion of reality television shows? Are they all hype or are there elements of truth to them?

6. Have there been times in your life when, like Drew, you had too much going on around you to hear God's voice clearly? What's the best remedy for times like that?

7. Is there a talent, like Janet's birdhouses, that you've been reluctant to share with the world?

Why? What steps can you take toward letting God use that talent?

8. Janet remembers "what seems too good to be true usually is." When has that been true in your life? Has it ever been wrong? Has something "too good to be true" really been good?

9. Has someone "let you down" the way Janet feels Drew has? What's the best response for a person of faith in a situation like that? What would you change now to your own response if you could?

10. Do you think Drew should have left the work site? Why or why not?

11. Middleburg has lots of interesting characters. Which remind you of yourself? Do you see other people in your life reflected in the book's characters?

12. Do you think Drew should have told Janet how he felt in Chapter Twenty-Three? Why or why not?

13. What would you have done with the check Drew gave Janet?

14. Drew decides God sent him into Janet's life to help her heal. Has God sent someone into your life to help them heal? What does it feel like you should be doing to help that person— and what's best left up to God in that situation?

15. Are you too busy fixing things to stop and fix yourself? What can you do about that?

*Turn the page for a sneak peek of
RITA® Award-winner Linda Goodnight's
heartwarming story,
HOME TO CROSSROADS RANCH.
On sale in March 2009
from Steeple Hill Love Inspired®.*

Chapter One

Nate Del Rio heard screams the minute he stepped out of his Ford F-150 SuperCrew and started up the flower-lined sidewalk leading to Rainy Jernagen's house. He double-checked the address scribbled on the back of a bill for horse feed. Sure enough, this was the place.

Adjusting his Stetson against a gust of March wind, he rang the doorbell, expecting the noise to subside. It didn't.

Somewhere inside the modest, tidy-looking brick house, at least two kids were screaming their heads off in what sounded to his experienced ears like fits of temper. A television blasted out Saturday morning cartoons—SpongeBob, he thought, though he was no expert on kids' television programs.

He punched the doorbell again. Instead of the

expected *ding-dong,* a raucous alternative Christian rock band added a few more decibels to the noise level.

Nate shifted the toolbox to his opposite hand and considered running for his life while he had the chance.

Too late. The bright red door whipped open. Nate's mouth fell open with it.

When the men's ministry coordinator from Bible Fellowship had called him, he'd somehow gotten the impression that he was coming to help a little old schoolteacher. You know, the kind that only drives to school and church and has a big, fat cat.

Not so. The woman standing before him with taffy-blond hair sprouting out from a disheveled ponytail couldn't possibly be any older than his own thirty-one years. A big blotch of something purple stained the front of her white sweatshirt and she was barefooted. Plus, she had a crying baby on each hip and a little red-haired girl hanging on one leg, bawling like a sick calf. And there wasn't a cat in sight.

What had he gotten himself into?

"May I help you?" she asked over the racket. Her blue-gray eyes were a little too unfocused and bewildered for his comfort.

Raising his voice, he asked, "Are you Ms. Jernagen?"

"Yes," she said cautiously. "I'm Rainy Jernagen. And you are…?"

"Nate Del Rio."

She blinked, uncomprehending, all the while jiggling both babies up and down. One grabbed a hank of her hair. She flinched, her head angling to one side as she said, still cautiously, "Okaaay."

Nate reached out and untwined the baby's sticky fingers.

A relieved smile rewarded him. "Thanks. Is there something I can help you with?"

He hefted the red toolbox to chest level so she could see it. "From the Handy Man Ministry. Jack Martin called. Said you had a washer problem."

Understanding dawned. "Oh, my goodness. Yes. I'm so sorry. You aren't what I expected. Please forgive me."

She wasn't what he expected either. Not in the least. Young and with a houseful of kids. He suppressed a shiver. No wonder she looked like the north end of a southbound cow. Kids, even grown ones, could drive a person to distraction. He should know. His adult sister and brother were, at this moment, making his life as miserable as possible. The worst part was they did it all the time. Only this morning his sister, Janine, had finally packed up and gone back to Sal, giving Nate a few days' reprieve.

"Come in, come in," the woman was saying. "It's been a crazy morning what with the babies showing up at three a.m. and Katie having a sick stomach. Then while I was doing the laundry, the washing machine went crazy. Water everywhere." She jerked her chin toward the inside of the house. "You're truly a godsend."

He wasn't so sure about that, but he'd signed up for his church's ministry to help single women and the elderly with those pesky little handyman chores like oil changes and leaky faucets. Most of his visits had been to older ladies who plied him with sweet tea and jars of homemade jam and talked about the good old days while he replaced a fuse or unstopped the sink. And their houses had been quiet. Real quiet.

Rainy Jernagen stepped back, motioned him in, and Nate very cautiously entered a room that should have had flashing red lights and a *danger zone* sign.

Toys littered the living room like Christmas morning. An overturned cereal bowl flowed milk onto a coffee table. Next to a playpen crowding one wall, a green package belched out disposable diapers. Similarly, baby clothes were strewn, along with a couple of kids, on the couch and floor. In a word, the place was a wreck.

"The washer is back this way behind the kitchen. Watch your step. It's slippery."

More than slippery. Nate kicked his way through the living room and the kitchen area beyond, though the kitchen actually appeared much tidier than the rest, other than the slow seepage of water coming from somewhere beyond. The shine of liquid glistening on beige tile led them straight to the utility room.

"I turned the faucets off behind the washer when this first started, but a tubful still managed to pump out onto the floor." She hoisted the babies higher on her hip and spoke to a young boy sitting in the floor. "Joshua, get out of those suds."

"But they're pretty, Miss Rainy." The brown-haired boy with bright blue eyes grinned up at her, extending a handful of bubbles. Light reflected off each droplet. "See the rainbows? There's always a rainbow, like you said. A rainbow behind the rain."

Miss Rainy smiled at the child. "Yes, there is. But right now, Mr. Del Rio needs in here to fix the washer. It's a little crowded for all of us." She was right about that. The space was no bigger than a small bathroom. "Can I get you to take the babies to the playpen while I show him around?"

"I'll take them, Miss Rainy." An older boy with a serious face and brown plastic glasses entered the room. Treading carefully, he came forward and took both babies, holding them against his slight chest. Another child appeared behind him. This one a girl with very blond hair and eyes the exact blue of the boy's, the one she'd called Joshua. How many children did this woman have, anyway? Six?

A heavy, smothery feeling pressed against his airway. Six kids?

Before he could dwell on that disturbing thought, a scream of sonic proportions rent the soap-fragrant air. He whipped around ready to protect and defend.

The little blond girl and the redhead were going at it.

"It's mine." Blondie tugged hard on a Barbie doll.

"It's mine. Will said so." To add emphasis to her demand, the redhead screamed bloody murder. "Miss Rainy."

About that time, Joshua decided to skate across the suds, and then slammed into the far wall next to a door that probably opened into the garage. He grabbed his big toe and set up a howl. Water sloshed as Rainy rushed forward and gathered him into her arms.

"Rainy!" Blondie screamed again.

"Rainy!" the redhead yelled.

Nate cast a glance at the garage exit and considered a fast escape.

Lord, I'm here to do a good thing. Can You help me out a little?

Rainy, her clothes now wet, somehow managed to take the doll from the fighting girls while snuggling Joshua against her side. The serious-looking boy stood in the doorway, a baby on each hip, taking in the chaos.

"Come on, Emma," the boy said to Blondie. "I'll make you some chocolate milk." So they went, slip-sliding out of the flooded room.

Four down, two to go.

Nate clunked his toolbox onto the washer and tried to ignore the chaos. Not an easy task, but one he'd learned to deal with as a boy. As an adult, he did everything possible to avoid this kind of madness. The Lord had a sense of humor sending him to this particular house.

"I apologize, Mr. Del Rio," Rainy said, shoving at the wads of hair that hung around her face like Spanish moss.

"Call me Nate. I'm not that much older than you." At thirty-one and the long-time patriarch of his family, he might feel seventy, but he wasn't.

"Okay, Nate. And I'm Rainy. Really, it's not usually this bad. I can't thank you enough for coming over. I tried to get a plumber, but being Saturday…" she shrugged, letting the obvious go unsaid. No one could get a plumber on the weekend.

"No problem." He removed his white Stetson and placed it next to the toolbox. What was he supposed to say? That he loved wading in dirty soap suds and listening to kids scream and cry? Not likely.

Rainy stood with an arm around each of the remaining children—the rainbow boy and the redhead. Her look of embarrassment had him feeling sorry for her. All these kids and no man around to help. With this many, she'd never find another husband, he was sure of that. Who would willingly take on a boatload of kids?

After a minute, Rainy and the remaining pair left the room and he got to work. Wiggling the machine away from the wall wasn't easy. Even with all the water on the floor, a significant amount remained in the tub. This leftover liquid sloshed and gushed at regular intervals. In minutes, his boots were dark with moisture. No problem there. As a rancher, his boots were often dark with lots of things, the best of which was water.

On his haunches, he surveyed the back of the machine, where hoses and cords and metal parts twined together like a nest of water moccasins.

As he investigated each hose in turn, he once more felt a presence in the room. Pivoting on his heels, he discovered the two boys squatted beside him, attention glued to the back of the washer.

"A busted hose?" the oldest one asked, pushing up his glasses.

"Most likely."

"I coulda fixed it but Rainy wouldn't let me."

"That so?"

"Yeah. Maybe. If someone would show me."

Nate suppressed a smile. "What's your name?"

"Will. This here's my brother, Joshua." He yanked a thumb at the younger one. "He's nine. I'm eleven. You go to Miss Rainy's church?"

"I do, but it's a big church. I don't think we've met before."

"She's nice. Most of the time. She never hits us or anything, and we've been here for six months."

It occurred to Nate then that these were not Rainy's children. The kids called her Miss Rainy, not Mom, and according to Will they had not been here forever. But what was a young, single woman doing with all these kids?

* * * * *

Look for
HOME TO CROSSROADS RANCH
by Linda Goodnight,
on sale March 2009 only from
Steeple Hill Love Inspired®,
available wherever books are sold.

Love Inspired® SUSPENSE

RIVETING INSPIRATIONAL ROMANCE

Watch for our new series of
edge-of-your-seat suspense novels.
These contemporary tales
of intrigue and romance
feature Christian characters
facing challenges to their faith...
and their lives!

Steeple
Hill®

Visit:
www.SteepleHill.com

LISUSDIR07R